My name is Happy Farmer.

I was born in a cherry red 1967 Mercury Montclair near a strip mall outside Cooperstown, NY, not much more than fifty years ago, to a loving young couple who—at the time—had no money but who had very large dreams.

Their last name was Farmer.

They named me "Happy" after my mother's favorite children's book, *The Happy Farmer*. The Happy Farmer himself was a tall and jolly man who always dressed in happy-blue farmer's coveralls, through whose shoulder straps he always inserted his happy thumbs, and he always wore a very, very happy farmer's grin which said, in essence, I'm the happy farmer. I grow happy food that makes all good little boys and girls grow into good and happy adults.

In time, the blue canoe will repair itself. I know this as well as I know my excesses, which have been legion. The blue canoe is a living thing. In its way, it breathes, ages, knows much. It knows about trees and grasses. It knows about the atmosphere, rain and wind, thunder and sleet and fog. And it knows about the constellations that parade across the sky, night and day—Cassiopeia, Andromeda, the Big Dipper.

blue canoe

t.m. wright

blue canoe

a memoir of the newly non-corporeal

introduction by tom piccirilli

2009

for Roxane, with love

introduction

by tom piccirilli

Okay, so I'll fess up right here. I'm a hardcore admirer and devotee of T.M. Wright.

But of course that's not much of a confession. You'd expect the guy doing the introduction to be a major fan of the author in question. You'd expect them to have some history together, to have shared a few beers, helped each other out on occasion, all that good buddy-buddy stuff.

Traditionally you start an intro off in one of several ways. By *a)* discussing when you first read the author being introduced *b)* giving some cute anecdote or relevant personal information *c)* offering outright praise or *d)* breaking down the book and presenting some kind of synopsis of the story itself.

So *a)* I can't recall when I first read T.M. Wright's fiction. It was probably *A Manhattan Ghost Story* back in the '80s, but who the hell remembers the '80s, much less what you read in the '80s? Sadly not me. I wish I could chalk this up to good drugs, but I was a boring shit then, same as I am now, except I'm an older boring shit now, and that's what we can chalk my faulty memory up to.

And *b)* I've only met Terry a couple of times in person and despite me considering him a friend, I have no interesting or humorous anecdotes to share. See the a) response if you want to know why.

Onto *c)* The praise. We started with that, remember? I'm introducing the book, so my praise and respect for T.M. Wright is rather implicit right there, isn't it? You don't introduce a book you hate by a writer you despise. The love is obvious, ain't it? Besides, we'll get to all the kind words in a little while. That's what the body of the introduction itself is all about, dig? So hold on.

All right, we're at *d)* And that's probably the roughest way to tackle this thing. For the past twenty minutes I've been sitting here at my desk staring at an empty screen trying to come up with some kind of synopsis for *Blue Canoe*, the fascinating book which you're about to read. I've failed and that really irks me. I'm supposed to be able to explain myself adequately if nothing more.

So anyhow, I'm out of avenues in which to start off this intro-duction, but, ta-da, we're already well underway, so it worked.

It isn't easy writing an introduction to T.M. Wright's fiction. In fact, it's damned difficult. Just check out Ramsey Campbell's intro to *I Am The Bird*, or Jack Ketchum's intro to the signed hardcover limited edition of *Strange Seed*. You think this right here is weird? Just go read them. Those guys really blew their corks. This intro that you're getting from me, well hell, this is *sensible* in comparison.

I have a theory about why it's so hard to do an intro to Terry's work.

T.M. Wright's style is the kind that all writers aspire to. He manages to convey real emotion about the most abstract and ambitious subject matter. He writes about the deepest meaning behind such important topics as family, love, the arc of our lives, the arc of our deaths, the fear of what awaits us in the afterworld, the terror of what we might bring with us and what we might leave behind forever.

Listen, when you read a chapter in *Blue Canoe* with the sub-heading *Epistobel and the Continuing Dissolution of Subatomic Structures*, you know you're entering some strange territory. When Terry does it, it feels authentic, natural, and valid. But when we write *about* him writing about it, then it's easy to slip gears and go wheeling into literary freefall.

One of the strengths of Terry Wright's fiction is that it defies expectations even after you've read his work. You expect that you'll be able to tell a friend, "You've got to check this book out, it's brilliant, it's amazing." And you will say that, trust me. But when your buddy asks, "Well, what's it about?" you'll realize just how hard it is to break down the poetry, the oddity, the creativity of it into something easily translated. You might even sit there for twenty minutes just staring like a mook, and your friend will probably wander away and not call you for some time.

But it's cheating if I don't even try, so here goes:

Blue Canoe may or may not be about a guy who may or may not be named Happy Farmer or MOMNB named Andrew Grimm who is or maybe isn't either dead or insane and WIOMI surrounded by ghosts or maybe nurses in a nuthatch or perhaps someone else, and WIOMI being haunted by his ex-girlfriend WIOMI named Epistobel WIOMI dead, alive, an amalgam of many girlfriends, a figment, a hallucination, or a phantasm. There is also a dog named *the-dog-who-would-have-been-Bob-had-he-been-Bob.*

The beautiful thing?

It all works. It all pulls together in a wonderful, poignant, thoughtful, literate, impressive, and heart wrenching way. In the midst of all this poetic, insightful, disturbing oddity, you'll find an amazing amount of straight-up black humor. You'll snicker, chuckle, and maybe even titter throughout.

And you'll probably do it the way that I did—without fully knowing why something is so funny. It just hits you that way. You'll get whiplash by how quickly you're whisked from some dark unsettling scene to a quick aside that will make you knock out a belly laugh.

You'll be stunned, amazed, cheered, warmed, and seriously spooked by *Blue Canoe*, kids. Just turn the page and discover that for yourself.

Now please excuse me. I have to go phone a friend and see if I can get him to talk to me again.

Tom Piccirilli
January, 2009

blue canoe

a memoir of the newly non-corporeal

begins

Not long after my father passed away, I found a brief and cryptic letter in one of the drawers of his huge roll-top desk. It read:

Dear Son,

> *There are times in our lives (some of us, not all of us) when our memories (the things we actually remember) become unreliable.*

> *All my love.*

He did not sign it.

Do you know about the constellations? I do. The Big Dipper, Orion, Cassiopeia, Andromeda (and its captive spiral galaxy, the only other galaxy beyond our own Milky Way Galaxy that we on Earth can see with the naked eye). The constellations are fantastic stories written in the night sky.

I read these stories often.

ii

The locals call it a mountain, but it's simply a tall, tree-covered hill, like all the mountains in the area, and when I look at it from the window in the oblong room where I've done my work for many years I know I'll climb it eventually, though I haven't climbed a hill of any size since I hit my forties and the demons of age began lumbering after me.

It's surprising what I do when I'm alone, though I won't, at this moment, share what it is I do. Shit, sometimes even *I* don't remember, which makes me sad because I think maybe I'm in early Alzheimer's, or experiencing a terminal kind of denial (perhaps, at some point, I'll deny my own existence and the universe will be done with me.)

I'm not a loon. The world is filled to overflowing with loons and I'm not one of them.

ii

Perhaps you don't like Roman numerals. If so, stay away. Roman numerals are the pillars of our modern civilization.

iii

Here it is, what this is all about: something more than woodchucks and deer exists on that tall hill and I'm going to find it.

Don't get me wrong. I have no firsthand knowledge, have heard no rumors, read no reports, seen no lurid headlines. I'm mostly ignorant, and all but inept. But I know that when I leave this room and go there—to that hill, and climb it—I'll be rewarded.

I *need* a reward, all of us do—you and yours and all our friends and relations. We need a reward simply for existing, for remaining a part of the human race instead of willingly turning ourselves into ashes or fertilizer.

Around my large house, there are several tons of ashes and fertilizer and I know all the names and all the histories. It's like living in a huge open book that no one else bothers to read.

At this very moment, a large spider is making its way with great spider urgency (a slow urgency, full of spider arrogance) across my window screen. The spider is easily the size of a quarter and I'm happy it's on the opposite side of the screen. True, however, that spiders are masters of slipping in and out of places too small even for the very small, so . . .

It's comical and grisly watching the spider take flight: flick the screen with your middle finger, as if you're hitting a carom piece, and in a moment, the spider will vanish, *poof*, into spider nothingness.

It is the following day and the giant spider has not returned. I have rowed a blue canoe to the other side of the lake and stood on the other shore and looked up, at the tall hill and the trees and woodchucks, the deer and the other creatures who exist there who watch me watching nothing.

My eyes are alive with green. This is the green of the trees, like a great wall of green.

No one came with me in that canoe, though I saw others in rowboats and speed boats, and in those noisy one-person machines that slide along on top of the water as if they're afraid of it.

vi

Given enough time, nothing becomes what we would like it to be. Time is the great enemy, but it is, in fact—the others say—not a real enemy because it can't be overcome, and so it must be dealt with on its own terms, which are the only terms available to us. And I say to the others, "Fuck that! Oh, fuck that!" And the others grin, usually, or sigh, or grin and sigh and nod and shrug, and then proclaim, "Oh, well, what can you do?"

vii

I was nearly fifteen and Charlene was thirteen and I loved her so much I came to believe I must be someone very special (to be able to love so fully and completely), and she fell from a hayloft and cracked her pretty skull—didn't die, but didn't recognize me ever again, or want to, I think. She's somewhere, still, drawing breath.

Do you remember her eyes? Blue as deep water.

Of course you don't. How could you? This foolishness. It's like food, sometimes.

viii

The giant spider has not returned. It's clear he fell to his death against the hard earth two stories below my window (of five in this oblong room). Perhaps I'll look for him—he's doubtless been eaten by birds, though. That's the way the universe works. Spiders eat small insects, birds eat spiders, and so on. Who would say "poor spider"? Not I. Spiders, you will learn, are unlike humans because they have no soul. That is also true of larger animals who aren't human, such as all dogs and cats and great killer whales and all flying things—flying insects and the birds who feed on them, and bats, the only flying mammals. All of these creatures are part of a great and continuing cycle of life and death and resurrection, but are apart from humans in that continuing cycle, which is one, I hasten to add, that I witness day and night here, in this place.

Which is to say, as a small footnote, that we can all breathe a little easier when our darling Schnauzer or beloved Abyssinian shuffles off this mortal coil—you see, he's going nowhere but into the ground, the landfill, the pet-size black plastic garbage bag. And who hasn't seen enough of *that* to last into the next millennium?

In the sparse woods around my house, I see nothing much. During daylight, gray squirrels all in a dither about the coming autumn and, at night, an occasional moving shadow which, of course, has nothing to do with me or this house.

And now, from my window, I can see the blue canoe.

ix

My father continued:

> We are forgotten. We become merely lines and moving shadows, first, then only shadows, then shadows which fade. But here's the oddly important thing, Son: All of this is to our advantage; it helps us move along to where we desperately need to go, without the intrusion of the others who stay in that other place, who come to us weeping and whining and with fingers that grasp and hold and won't release.

two

She liked Edward Hopper, I liked Edward Hopper, she adored BB King, *I* adored BB King, she loathed canned salmon, I loathed it as well—oh, it was a fated confluence of similar souls.

Listen to her name: Epistobel. You've known no one by that name, don't even wrack your brain trying to remember. It was her mother's invention: she felt that it meant "flowing beauty," although, according to Epistobel herself, she had no reason for believing this, only that the name sounded as if it *should* mean "flowing beauty."

Is Epistobel a flowing beauty?

I don't remember.

ii

It's grievous and reprehensible to lie, though not to oneself, and if a man can learn to believe the lies he tells himself, those lies, in a world filled to the point of pain with the real, can become necessary to his survival.

Contrary to pedestrian belief, it's not only possible but true that we can ultimately define what's "real" by a simple, stubborn, and steady application of faith.

iii

I look left and right around the edges of the dark window shade; I see sunlight straining to enter the room and, try as I might, I cannot look away.

iv

Epistobel was no flowing beauty and that's a fact (in any realm, facts are mortally important. They ground us. We can't exist without them). She was difficult to look at, uncomfortable to be with, joyless, pitiless, too, and her libido was a thing she hardly ever used. It's remarkable that I let her come into my life and stay in it for as long as she apparently did. Good lord, it may have been years!

Even now, I can recall her so well that I actually see her moving about in this room, in the woods around the house, in the house itself. I even imagined, recently, that she sat with me in the blue canoe while I rowed to the opposite shore.

She had a curious odor—herbal, perhaps thyme. It wasn't unpleasant or cloying, it was simply an odor, though it permeated our encounters.

She never raised her voice. It wasn't a monotone—that would have been unbearable. It was simply that she never seemed to become angry, always choked it back, perhaps (and that's probably why she was so difficult to look at, now that I think about it; she was forever choking back her anger, letting it become part of her cartilage, muscle, and bone. After a while, all that anger puts pressure on the body and the body becomes twisted and unrecognizable).

It's not that she was homely. My guess is that she was far from homely, in fact. I'll even say this—if I were to have to look back at our relationship and actually see her face again, what I'd be looking at would be a rather pretty face, teeth and nose straight, eyes large and appealing, chin strong, skin flawless.

v

I'm going to tell you something and I want you to believe it:

I am no crazier than anyone you might see on the street or in an office, an elevator, at the laundromat, the pizza shop, the supermarket, the hospital waiting room, the used car lot, the little store on the corner that sells overpriced candy, the top floor of an old department store, a bus.

You must believe—I'm asking you to believe—that I have sat here many, many hours and pondered all the important questions you, too, have pondered, and, just like you, I've come up with no answers, simply more questions. Shit, that's the way it is; we aren't meant to find answers—what would be the use? It would simply make us contented in our ignorance.

The clock chimes. It's a wall clock in a dark case and it has the word "Regulator" on its face in gold script. It's key wound, with a simple *faux* brass pendulum that swings left/right, left/right in two-second intervals. It rests against the east wall—the rest of the wall is bare.

vi

Yes, actually, there *are* other people in this house.

vii

This is a large and comfortable room I'm in and I have no complaints. If I wanted, I could move to another room (there are many from which to choose, but none of them provide the view I have from this window. The other rooms look out on the thick woods behind the house, the narrow dirt driveway to the north, the gully to the south. Better simply to look through this window at the sparse woods, the narrow lake, the tall hill beyond, and, at night, at the great constellations which move with consummate grace from one horizon to the other and, in the process, tell their fantastic stories).

Tomorrow, I'll get into the canoe, again, row to the lake's opposite shore and find on the tall hill there whatever there is to find.

viii

It was I who painted the canoe. Its owner paid me to paint it, though he did not pay well; he paid me in meals—seven dinners and seven lunches at his small house on the lake. His name was Sid and he smelled of motor oil, though he stayed scrupulously clean.

He died without leaving a will, so the blue canoe sat on cinder blocks in front of his house for a couple of years before I came along and started to borrow it from time to time.

No one's moved into Sid's house. I've heard talk in the little village at the north end of the lake that his relatives are fighting over the acreage—lakefront property goes for a pretty penny here. But the relatives are making a long affair of it and, I've been told, settling everything in probate could take years.

So, I borrow the canoe a couple of times a week. Mostly, I just row along the lakeshore for an hour or so. It's good exercise, and the view is pleasant, at times it's even stimulating.

I didn't much care for Sid, perhaps because he was stingy and scrupulously clean and smelled of oil. His loss means little to me; perhaps, after all, it means nothing.

If that's true—that his death means nothing to me—then I'm pleased. After all, death is a thing which cannot be argued, debated, pleaded with or defeated because, in point of *fact*, it isn't a *thing* at all. It's merely a stopping point. It's the end of a song or the end of a long sentence or of a novel or a billion inhales and exhales which will never be repeated.

ix

It *is* true that there are others in this house.

x

They pay my bills and prepare my meals. They take turns at that—meal preparation—because my dietary needs are complex and extreme due to allergies, and preparing a really tasty meal is difficult at best—even I can't do it and, in my day, I was a passable chef.

There are animals in the house, too. It can't be said that they're pets, most of them, because they come and go as they please and the others in the house don't tend to their needs. These animals include two raccoons (adults; a male and a female, I believe, though I have no idea how to determine the sex of a raccoon [beyond picking one up by its hind feet and having a look]), perhaps as many as half a dozen chipmunks, a coyote whose presence is more a matter of divination than actually viewing, a number of bats who fly past my door at dusk and at dawn, a cat which the others have named Lilliputian (he's as big as a Jack Russell terrier and just as mean), and a small, feral dog I have not named, though he seems, in his miserable, vulnerable way, to beg for a name, and affection. I doubt that's a complete list of the animals in the house (I won't mention the insects, which are numerous and insistent). I haven't visited the cellar or all of the attics to see what lives in them, but I've been told—by the others—that they believe a red fox has made a den in one of the third-floor bedrooms.

I'm especially fond of red foxes.

xi

As to the things I do when I'm alone—you must give me time to remember them and, upon remembering, to decide which of them are worth remembering, meaning which of them might entertain you.

That is, after all, the purpose of this narrative. To entertain. And remember.

xii

I've found a small hole in the blue canoe. Some years ago, I would have thrown a hell of a tantrum over such a discovery, but not today. Today I merely looked at the hole, gauged its severity and set about plugging it. It's not an important hole; it's just below the port gunwale, is about the size of a quarter, smooth-edged, and easy to repair with the proper patching material.

So I went into the village named after the lake and bought patching material.

A woman saw me at the store where I bought the patching material. She was tall and thin, attractive in a cunning, lean way, and she claimed I knew her.

I didn't know her, however.

The blue canoe has been patched.

Again, it's ready for use.

xiii

Oh, this is tiresome—the constant ringing of the telephone, the constant knocking at the doors and windows, the continual shouts from below—"What are you doing, for God's sake?" and, "Answer the fucking door!" and "What are you doing in there?"

And it's not simply one person who's responsible for this harassment, it's several, I'm sure—a man, a woman, a child (boy, girl—I don't know: I never catch a glimpse of her or him; I only hear a shrill high tenor voice: "Please come down! Please come down!").

I can tell you this much: I haven't always been harassed by these people—I would remember, but I remember only that, for years, now, my existence here has been peaceful, contented, without bother or tension. And now, for whatever reason, I'm being harassed.

xiv

I made my way to the blue canoe and across the narrow lake to the opposite shore, then several hundred feet up the tall hill, to where the woods grow thick enough that the light is constantly muted. It is mostly pines on that hill. Some maples and a scattering of tulip trees, yes, but mostly old and stately pines.

I saw a tall man in green and red peering at me from between two pines at a good shouting distance (I believe he was a hunter, though I doubt this is hunting season), but he was quickly on his way, followed by a black and white dog that seemed to pay me no attention.

Of course, that hill isn't inhabited, except in late autumn and in winter by hunters and, at other times, by hikers.

Dad (bless him, damn him) was a hunter. He killed a thousand and more animals of all sizes in his 68 years. He said, "Man should hunt because it's in the noblest traditions of his gender."

He hunted with a scruffy brown dog named Gator, who bit him five or six times a year, which was all right, Dad said, because Gator, like Dad himself, was only doing what his DNA told him to do.

I never went hunting with him. He invited me often, but I always declined. He gave up inviting me when I was a young teenager. He said, "Shit then, I guess you'll live the way you think you ought to."

I remember Dad's face, but not his voice, which, in my memory, is nevertheless like the bark of a bullfrog.

three

i

It's not that meals are prepared for me and then brought up here, to this room, by servants. It's not that way at all. Not anymore. I recall, however, a beautiful young woman who brought me good, nutritious meals periodically. She had a name, of course, though I don't remember it. I remember much, but I have forgotten much, too. It's what time does to all of us, and that's a fact.

ii

I love broccoli, an unapologetic vegetable, such a hearty, tangy taste that does not (like asparagus) insinuate itself upon the urine . And good cheeses—Brie, for instance, and Camembert, Neufchâtel, Ricotta. The tongue is made for the texture of warm cheese, wouldn't you agree? And the palate is made for its varied tastes—startling, succulent, sweet, as subtle as candlelight.

My father ate cheese at every meal (meat, as well). He claimed that it soothed his temperament. He is, now—at this stage in my existence, and in my pitiful imaginings and memory—little more than a tall, large-headed man in a baggy gray suit who's standing in shadow. Sometimes, in this imagining, he turns his head and smiles in the way he often smiled at me (as if he knew something about me that I didn't), but, usually, I see only his profile. In this imagining, his skin is as gray as the clothes he wears, a cigarette dangles from his mouth (though he never smoked) and his hands are thrust into his pants pockets. He never speaks in these imaginings. It's doubtful, at any rate, that I would remember his voice.

iii

I look forward, now, to the occasional appearance of the feral dog in my doorway. I've almost decided to befriend him, should he make the first move. Dogs have played a huge part in my life, as I recall. (And they still do, of course, though in ways that are, I'm beginning to suspect, necessarily at right angles to the parts they once played.) I remember dogs of various sizes, colors, personalities: all of them lived long lives with great energy. I buried some of them personally; others were spirited away by people who meant well.

iv

Epistobel had three cats, all calico, all female. One was unfriendly and the other two were not. One was blind.

v

Shit, this is no rational way to spend these short days and long nights—locked up in memory.

Fuck the blue canoe!

A plague of regret waits there, on that tall hill.

And myriad questions, too.

I don't remember Epistobel. That's not her name, anyway. I don't remember her name. I know only that it wasn't "Epistobel." Such a stupid name. Who would curse his child with such a name? Who would doom his child to a lifetime of "Epistobel? Epistobel?" It's as cumbersome as a deep pocket full of small change.

vi

Believe this, it's important: I do indeed leave this room and go elsewhere, sometimes to the village that bears the name of the lake, and sometimes elsewhere, to the tall hill, for instance, though I've been there only twice.

Of course, you doubt me, which is both the strength and weakness of this narrative—its very uncertainty and ambiguity. I know that.

My name is Happy Farmer.

I was born in a cherry-red 1967 Mercury Montclair near a strip mall outside Cooperstown, NY, not much more than fifty years ago, to a loving young couple whose very large dreams took the place of money.

Their last name was Farmer.

They named me "Happy" after my mother's favorite children's book, *The Happy Farmer*, a tall and jolly man who always dressed in happy-blue farmer's coveralls, through whose shoulder straps he always inserted his happy thumbs, and he always wore a very, very happy farmer's grin, which said, in essence, *I'm the happy farmer. I grow happy food that makes all good little boys and girls grow into good and happy adults.*

That may be a misinterpretation of the Happy Farmer's motivations. Perhaps he was just happy he'd cleaned up the pig shit (worst smell in the universe) and emptied happy Bessie's bursting teats.

Sure, I'll allow him that.

This Happy Farmer, however, has acquired a gigantic red can of Raid ("Kills Bugs Dead!") Flying Insect, Ant and Spider Killer because the quarter-size spider I thought I'd dispatched not too long ago has enlisted the aid of at least a hundred of his horrific buddies, and they're crowding my window screen *en masse*. For Jesus Hopping Christ, I can barely see the lake and the tall hill through the screen. It's a horror show, for sure. But my chemical offensive should drive them off, at least—and send most of them to that great and tangled web in the sky, too.

Ha!

vi

We do not live to kill. We live to survive. If we don't survive, we don't live; that seems obvious (so much seems obvious, now). And if we don't live, it's clear we continue to exist as the mega-dimensional, unpredictable and irascible victims of unavoidable circumstance.

That's something someone—whose name I don't remember—once told me. I think it's profound.

I wasn't born in a 1967 Mercury Montclair. How would that have been possible, and how could you believe it? What's today's date, after all? Go and check. Have you returned? Good. Then you can see, shit, that not enough *time* (the great emancipator) has passed.

What are you, stupid?

I was born in the backseat of a dark green, 1947 Hudson Hornet. It is possible, I'll be quick to add, that I wasn't actually *born* there, merely conceived there, in that backseat.

And Epistobel?

What of her? She existed, certainly. Who can deny it?

Not I. Though I do. Though I do. *(I grow old, I grow old, I grow repetitious.)*

vii

Well, of course, we deny many, many things—our age, our weight, the ordinariness of our IQ, our gluttonous or unhealthy eating habits, our tv-watching habits ("Oh, you know, I don't really watch television—only PBS!"), driving habits, bad habits (picking our nose, scratching our ass, farting, belching, interrupting, going without a bath or shower for weeks at a time, becoming non-corporeal at altogether inconvenient moments). This is how we get along in a universe which—you know—expects way too fucking much of us. And the end-product of all that necessary denial? We tell ourselves we're good at practically everything we do, or, at least, that we're competent at it or, at the very least, that we're still learning (we call ourselves "a work in progress").

Take lovemaking.

All of us believe we're good at it. And what is our criteria for being "good" at it? It's whether we have an orgasm. Some more enlightened souls rate good lovemaking as producing an orgasm in our partner. Well, that's very generous, very giving. And very anti-natural. It's not up to us, for Christ's sake, to worry about our partner's orgasm—that's *his* or *her* department. Shit, we've got our own orgasm to worry about if we're going to keep the planet populated, which is, after all, the purpose of fucking.

And it isn't "lovemaking," or "lust," or "carnal knowledge," or "getting your ashes hauled." It's *fucking*. Shit, it's what one little terrier does to the other little terrier, what the stallion does to the mare, what horny octopi do to other horny octopi.

But it is not, I hasten to add, what Epistobel and I did to one another.

I can support that.

viii

An excellent breakfast this morning. Good runny eggs with potato bread toast layered with orange marmalade and butter, followed by a glass of freshly squeezed mango/kiwi juice that got my gut really singing.

"Thank you so much for this," I said to the young lady who brought it to me.

"Our pleasure, sir," she said, and backed out of the room.

I don't like that backing out of the room stuff. It's an affectation.

ix

One of the things I do when I'm alone is play with my navel. I stick my finger in and move it around and then look at it, expecting, I think, to see something unusual. But that never happens.

x

It's later, now. I've been thinking about these goddamned Roman numerals and have decided to stop using them. I hope you don't mind.

xi

Another thing I do when I'm alone is take off my clothes and look at my body in a tall mirror which hangs, apparently, on the back of my closet door. The mirror is imperfect and it makes my body look convex or concave in spots, like a funhouse mirror, though not nearly as exaggerated. If I stand just so about six feet in front of this tall mirror, I can make my cock look quite large and my belly quite small. This is perfect for middle-age men who have not been taking care of themselves.

⊶

Epistobel and I approached lovemaking as if it were something lethal.

That's quite a statement, I know. I wish I could explain it. I can't. The word "lethal" simply leapt from my fingers when I'd finished with the word "something," so what could I do? "Lethal," "mortal," "non-corporeal"—these words buzz about me like flies.

I suppose I could surmise that the act of lovemaking, when it's "good," produces orgasms, and that orgasms are first cousins to death itself (if they're done right, I think: sometimes, during an orgasm, I can scream and rant and rave and push and push and push and grunt and sweat in earnest, honestly, and, at the same time, I can think about some piece of work I'm involved with, a blemish on the wall behind the bed, my partner's nose (a tad crooked, a bit too long, abnormally clogged, the slight presence of blood, perhaps): such orgasms have no familial relationship to death whatever, but orgasms that are minus these distractions, that are composed completely of grunts and groans, sweat, shock and paralysis are, indeed, cousins to death: you will ask me why, and, in time, I think I shall tell you, because, in time, I'm sure I'll *know* why).

i

"Please don't back out of the room," I beseeched the comely young woman who brought my breakfast.

"Of course," she said, but continued backing out of the room.

"It just seems so . . . archaic," I said. "It makes me feel like a potentate."

She stopped; she was near the door. She cocked her head: "Potentate?"

"Sure. Royalty. Like royalty," I said. "A king or a prince or something."

"But you're none of those things," she said, and cocked her head the other way. She has a pretty head and a consumable body.

"Listen," I said, "when you bring me my breakfast, next time . . ."

She vanished.

That's the way it happens, now. Blame the excesses of time. You see, if you exceed the normal flow of time, because you're not paying attention, or you're ignoring the moment, the minute, the hour, the entire fucking day, so you're moving through time almost as if it didn't exist—I've learned this over many years—then the time that's supposed to happen just ahead of where you are now becomes compressed. It's the same sort of thing that happens when a jet flies faster than the speed of sound. But, instead of producing a sonic boom, *time*—tripping all over itself, moving faster and faster and faster, still—does something else. It eliminates the near future just ahead of it.

And that's what happened. I'm sure of it.

That's where the comely young woman went.

Into some non-existent near-future.

iii

I went to the blue canoe and put it into the water and sat in it near the shore—perhaps for an hour, perhaps two hours, perhaps for as many as three or four hours—and went nowhere.

Sunny day. Not the kind of day I normally like. But the air was as still as death and the lake reflected the sunlight and I felt that going anywhere in the blue canoe would have been futile.

I sat in the canoe for some time. Perhaps many hours. A raccoon came by at some point and looked at me for a couple of minutes from the sandy shore, got up on its hind legs and pawed the air. It seemed to me that he was asking a question, but I said nothing. Eventually, he lumbered off, chattering a little. And I continued sitting in the blue canoe.

At last, I came back here. To this house. And this oblong room.

iii

Epistobel knew nothing of my pain and I knew everything of hers.

We lived in the same house, in different rooms, and, on some days, she'd flit from here to there, avoiding me, and, on other days, I'd lumber here and lumber there, avoiding her. What a clumsy and uncomfortable and abusive way to carry on a relationship. It's amazing we agreed to it. Amazing we ever came together. Amazing we gave each other a thousand and more orgasms (I always attended like a servant to her orgasms and she did the same for mine: usually, it was she who had the first orgasm, and then I would have my (one) orgasm, and she would have another—because of my orgasm—and then another, and another, and I found myself watching her using all that orgasmic energy and envying her and wanting, at the same time, to scream, "God, I'm done, Epistobel, I'm done, so can I please just lie down now and watch *you?*" I never said that, of course. It would have been rude.

And, of course, I'm not rude. Or a loon. Or alone. Blessedly, damnably *not* alone.

Well, yes, you see, they're everywhere. The others and the animals—the terrier who is as-yet unnamed, and the cat named

Lilliputian, and the insects, the spiders, all the bats flitting here and flitting there at dusk and dawn.

You're asking yourself now, *Which of all this is fantasy and which is reality?* And I could be very cavalier and answer, "Well, who really knows the difference between the two—between fantasy and reality?" And that would make you stop and ponder and, after a while, admit that I'm right (some of you), or accuse me of sophistry (others of you) or, worse, that I'm fobbing off a cliché as something profound (which is what Epistobel would have said).

But when you really get down to it, when you start rubbing your nose in it, begin licking it, eating it, masticating it, ingesting it, digesting it, who really *does* know the differences between reality and fantasy?

Certainly not I. And I'm not even a loon.

iv

I read a short-short story from *The Collected Works of Edgar Allan Poe* last night; it was titled "Silence, A Fable," and I read it a couple of times because it was so transporting and I needed to be transported, even though the place to which it transported me was one which I would never visit in reality, a place where I kept company with a taciturn and frightening man.

And where do *you* go when you must go somewhere?

To *this* place? If so, what place *is* this?

v

The sun on the mist this morning is blinding and I can't look at it for more than a second or two, when I have to turn away, close the heavy shade, sit in darkness.No light is visible under my closed door.

And there is only one window.

I believe, sometimes, that if I sit in darkness long enough, then, at last, open the heavy shade, or go to my door and open it, I'll discover that, during my absence from the world of light (the world I once inhabited) a new world has emerged, a world I don't recognize—and it's a fantastic world full of fantastical people and animals and situations—existence-in-the-balance situations, for instance, or (less likely, I hope) it's a world of the mundane, or a world so profoundly unrecognizable I simply can't react to it because nothing in my memories or my genetics can tell me how to react to it—to run from it or embrace it or discover it or simply to close the room-darkening shade again, or the door. And let darkness do the soothing thing it has always done.

The clock chimes.

four

I've discovered a very small village or hamlet near the middle of the tall hill across the lake, and it's a village or hamlet I'm sure the inhabitants of the town named after the lake do not know exists.

ii

I believe this because the very small village is at least a dozen miles from the town named after the lake and has been built in a very isolated place on the tall hill, in an unusually dense pine forest redolent with the scent of pine and the portentous and heavy weight of silence. As well, there was quite a number of what looked like the thin, hemp-colored garlands one associates with live oaks hanging from these pines, as if in early celebration of Christmas, although there was nothing festive about them.

I should tell you, as well, that there were no people in the village (I'll call it a village, rather than a hamlet: I'm not sure of the difference between the two—"a very small village" and "a hamlet"—but I prefer the word "village," because it seems warmer and, hence, more inviting, although that certainly doesn't describe this village accurately), though there were signs that people did indeed live there.

iii

It's possible, also, that I heard occasional voices from within the thick pine forest. Of course, these could have been the chattering and twittering of squirrels and raccoons; I heard no words, only the various pitches of various voices on the still air.

iv

They persist, the man and woman who, by turns, whisper and talk loudly to me from below, the phone calls, the child who pleads—in words I can't understand because they're unintelligible—from beyond my closed door. I should notify someone about them, perhaps. During this odd harangue, I tell myself that I should call the police or the county sheriff. File a complaint. But, soon enough, the ringing phone stops ringing and all the people go away.

v

I don't believe I want to lie to you about Epistobel. Or deceive you, manipulate the truth, lay down red herrings.

I'll tell you this, however: Epistobel exists. As much as this room exists, as much as the mean-as-spit cat, Lilliputian, exists, and the tiny village on the tall hill across the lake (where, I'm certain, dreamers are).

All these are facts, and my problem now (and for the past I- don't-know-how-many years) is how to deal with these facts in a way that will keep me from exiting the stage.

vi

I'm so sorry for that, for engaging in a bit of oddly self-aggrandizing melodrama. I apologize. When you start writing a fantasy such as this, melodrama naturally creeps into your narrative. Believe me, I am in no way close to exiting the stage—either by choice, illness, or accident.

I am, I'm all but certain, merely amusing myself in this large, unventilated, dark and oblong room. I'm simply writing, I firmly believe, a fantasy about a fantasy woman who came and went from my life so many times it was necessary to deny not only her existence but, oddly, my own. ("Happy," my father once said [looking, then, like a large and magnificent bird of prey, perched at his tall window and framed by bright sky] "if you deny your existence you will stop believing. And then, of course, you will cease to exist.")

Of course, Epistobel never existed.

She exists, now, only here, in this room, through my fingers and my imaginings.

She exists when I do not rush through time and push aside what wants or needs to be in the moment that lies just ahead of the moment in which I actually exist.

Well, all of us need fantasy. We need it in the same way—to the same degree—that we need food, sunshine, rain and sympathy. (In an unusually lucid moment during her nightmarish 42nd year, my mother said, "Happy, we are warmed most by what smolders at our very core—and that is a place deep within the dense bone that allows us to walk and reach and *believe*.")

vii

Yes, I've been to that village again, though I found little more than I found two days ago—half a dozen wooden cottages, drably painted, but otherwise, in good repair, a few dirt paths in and out of the place (through the thick pine forest). And again, too, I heard what sounded like voices from beyond the place (in the thick woods), but, as before, it could have been merely the twittering of squirrels and raccoons.

I also found a nicely handmade wooden cradle standing at the front door of one of the cottages, as if it were being offered as a gift, as if the inhabitants of the cottage were expecting a child and someone (anonymous) had built the cradle for them. The gesture was touching, and I laid my hands on the cradle and rocked it, imagined the child within it, then I returned reluctantly to the blue canoe, paddled across the lake, and came back to this room.

You know, you have a favorite aunt, or a cherished teacher, or a brother or sister who becomes—through all those miserable formative years—someone special to you, and then they leave, become non-corporeal, and what in the name of heaven do you do? What *can* you do? Retreat so earnestly and with such psychic force from the moment you're in that you encounter these people again, as they once were? It's like trying to make warm soup out of stale air.

viii

It's much later than when I last wrote: it's several hours later, in fact and, clearly, the sun has set. I have a gooseneck lamp on my desk and it helps me see.

I wanted to add that I did, indeed, recognize some of the voices I heard while I was in the tiny village on the hill. I heard no particular words, of course, but I recognized (though I could not name) several pitches and rhythms in the chorus of voices that surrounded me as I made my way from cottage to cottage, and even as I left the village and returned to the blue canoe.

Such voices are only a kind of aural illusion, of course—especially in such an odd setting as that little hamlet. One hears the twittering of small animals and so, quite naturally, one populates the forest with voices from the past, even though names and faces one might associate with those voices are just beyond the reach of memory.

I hate writing like that, as if desperately trying to convince myself of something I can't face directly—in this case, that these "voices" are actually more than I'm presuming them to be: shit, they were obviously the voices of raccoons, and chipmunks, and squirrels, and perhaps even larger animals—coyotes, for instance (who exist by the hundreds in this county), or black bears, harmless unless provoked. At times, I see all of these creatures everywhere.

It's so obvious: we find ourselves in a strange place, a place of mystery, like this oblong room, or that tiny village, and something inside us needs to populate it with *people* and, because it's easier to manufacture an aural hallucination than an optical one, we populate these places with voices from the past.

Dammit to hell. I've said all that already. I grow old, I grow old. Fucking spiders. Are back.

ix

I found the room where the fox makes its den. It's on the third floor, as rumor (from the others) suggested, halfway down an unlighted corridor that runs north/south. The room has no door, so the fox can come and go as it pleases. I didn't see the fox there, though I smelled it—a strong, musky odor I first smelled when I was a child and I nearly tripped over a vixen and its cubs in a thicket not far from our farmhouse.

I didn't go into the room where the fox makes its den. Perhaps, I reasoned, it's a female in estrous and insinuating my human odor on the room might scare her off.

There was a large, dark leather couch in the room, a four-drawer wooden file cabinet, a huge roll-top desk (in need of much repair) beside it, and a threadbare red and green and white oval oriental rug in front of the couch. I guessed that the fox used the right side of the couch as a bed because the cushion there was torn and the stuffing rearranged into a sort of nest.

x

When we first hear thunder, it's at such a distance we say, "Is that thunder?" and then we wait a moment, hear the thunder repeat, and we nod, almost certain of what we're hearing, but still not quite certain it isn't a truck on the interstate or an earth-moving machine carving out a hole. Then the thunder repeats a second time and we're sure now that it's thunder and we say, "I think a storm's coming." And if we like storms, we smile. And if we don't like storms, we sigh. Epistobel and I always smiled.

xi

But I don't hear thunder well in this room, with its one window, its thick walls, and the dense roof above.

xii

The others come here often, now—to this room. They hurry in and bustle about and hurry out, and I'm never quite sure what it is they've done when they're gone. I want to go to the door and call after them—their broad and slender backs—"What in God's name were you doing in my room?" but I know only too well I wouldn't get an answer, only, perhaps, a quick glance backward, the whisper of a smile.

xiii

My father wrote this, too (I remember it clearly): *"We human beings are as social as ants and, like ants, we die by the millions, but, Son, unlike ants, in that tortuous sleep after death, we dream of what it is to be more than simply one."*

xix

Oh yes, the blue canoe exists. It was manufactured by Tuft Industries, of Gary, Indiana. It's twelve feet long, two and a half feet wide at its widest point, and its original color was red, which you can see in quarter-inch wide strips just under the gunwales. Sid took good care of the canoe, stored it in a shed in the winter and, in the summer, kept it up on cinder blocks, under a tarp, so the sun wouldn't bleach the paint or buckle the wood (birch).

At times, when I'm in the canoe and rowing aimlessly, I feel a sudden *other* weight in it and I know that Sid himself has come back, from wherever death took him, to sit near me. I don't look for him, or see him, and he never talks.

xiv

Of course, I don't believe in ghosts, but they can be a comfort.

When we need a comfort. Perhaps we always need a comfort (especially when our oblong rooms offer no comfort whatever).

Epistobel once asked (I believe), "Do I comfort you?"

And oh, yes, she did. And comforts me now, as well—lingering on the edges of my dreams and the borders of my sleep, where (thankfully) I do not recognize her (because I will never recognize her, and *that's* a comfort; I recognize only that she needs to be there, or that I need her to be there, so, for God's sake, it *must* be her I'm seeing or sensing, just as it must be Sid I sense near me in the blue canoe).

Tuft Industries, Gary Indiana.

Elkhart Manufacturing, Joshua City, Nevada—the roll-top desk in the room where the fox has fashioned its den.

Phinney Walker—the makers of a small, brown leather-bound, travel alarm clock (circa 1947) that sits on my desk. It stopped working a year and a half ago; I keep it because it reminds me of what time truly is.

Hallmark—producers of the final greeting card I received from my mother—whose name was Grace—before her death: the card read, "Happy, leave the grieving to the ignorant, celebrate yourself. Mom." On the front of the card, there was a photograph of the face of a leopard frog; it took up the whole card—frog eyes and odd frog smile and the suggestion of frog toes around the edges. I saved the card for a while.

xv

It's late afternoon of another day, raining, and I've returned from the tiny village that sits partway up the tall hill. At the small cottage where I discovered the cradle, I found that the cradle was missing, but I could hear the insistent cries of an infant from within the cottage. The cries cheered me and I thought of knocking on the cottage's front door, though I could imagine no reason for disturbing its inhabitants. The care of a newborn is a nearly endless task and I decided my presence at that door would have been unwanted, so I made my way through the rest of the village, hoping, I think, to find evidence that others lived in it. But I found nothing.

That's always best, really. To find nothing.

I've learned that much, over time.

My mother said once, "Always leave well enough alone, Happy, and keep in mind that practically everything is *well enough*." She followed that with a quick, flat smile—one I'd grown used to but had never learned to interpret—and a quick nod, as if she were agreeing with herself.

I loved her because she was so troubled. She picked her nose in public, wore only a purple slip and a matching bra to do her gardening ("Happy, there's no problem. We have a fence, after all."), broke into fits of hysterical laughter at inappropriate times—at movie theaters, doctor's offices, during solemn events (Labor Day parades, funerals); she also brayed like a mule when she and Dad made love, and, since she insisted on keeping the windows open, the entire neighborhood (upper middle class, big houses, everyone's business was everyone's business) could hear, and sometimes, in my huge room on the house's third-floor, I heard occasional laughter from the other houses. When I went to school, I was sometimes greeted by anonymous braying noises from within the crowds of kids bustling here and bustling there.

High school was a nightmare, of course.

It's where, I believe, I met Epistobel.

Hers had been one of those anonymous, pretty faces for a year or so. Then I bled on her and the jaws of fate locked tight around both of us.

epistobel and the endless wait

My father wrote, "*Death will meet us on its own schedule, and so we must find a place that's comfortable and sane and we must plan to live in that place for many years. If we do that, Happy, then we'll know, at least, where we're going to die. So, each night in that place, before bed, we can look about at the things we've accumulated (letters, books, photographs, clocks, paintings, hats, galoshes and so forth) and know them for what they are—the sum of our lives—and we can nod and smile and be happy with them. It's not necessary to say goodnight to them, or goodbye to them, on a regular basis. We needn't assume each night, Happy, that we will not live past the morning. That, after all, is the great surprise that death has for us—the time of its visit. But, you see, we can handily choose the place, and, if we are careful about trips and traveling and the company we keep, we can know that Death will at last find us in a place we have chosen.*"

Here's the route to the blue canoe:

Descend three floors to the first floor, to the front door, turn right, follow a narrow path through a thick grove of pines and birches and the occasional maple until you come upon a mailbox (yes, in the middle of the growth of pines) stuck on a three-foot two-by-four, with the letters "I.G." scrawled on it in red, then make a left (north), which will lead you off the path momentarily, through a heavy growth of raspberry bushes (watch your face and arms; those little thorns can be painful), until you come to another, wider, path, where you turn right and follow the path through another pine grove for about half a mile until, all at once, the lake will be upon you and you'll see the blue canoe upside down on upturned cinder blocks.

Borrow it, if you wish. You'll discover it's capable of amazing things.

Epistobel and I swam together often. We never went out in a boat. She was afraid of boats, though not of swimming.

I waited quite a long time for her to touch me. And when it finally happened, it was maddeningly tentative, a touch on the forearm to punctuate something she'd just said, something about movies, or pets, or religion, I think—something not terribly profound, perhaps, though who can say now, so many years later?

I remember little of her. Not her face or her shape. Not even her voice, or her predilections—only (at this moment, rain is falling, random, jarring noises echoing through the house) her nose, which was small and unobtrusive.

ii

Hieronymus Bosch created some very nightmarish paintings, don't you think? He was a man caught in endless turmoil; clearly, he could eat his own soul and vomit it up. I've done such paintings as that, though not with the same success, of course: I've done them to illuminate my existence (prior to this moment, for no one but myself, but now for you, as well). Here's one of those paintings:

That was my house, to the left at the end of the street, beside the other two houses and behind the segmented streetlamp, very near the open-mouthed staring faces, the running men and screaming women.

If you look very closely into the darkness on the porch of that first house, you'll find Epistobel, too, her bright yellow dress flowing about her and her face turned from me (as usual).

I stare at this painting often, but I cannot see her. That's best. "It is preferable for us, of course, to always see nothing," my mother said. "Always, always. How much better for us if we had been born blind. They are truly blessed, you know—the blind. Truly. So when you look and do not see, thank whatever flotsam created you for your incredible lack of talent."

I remember growing up on mashed potatoes, creamed corn, spinach, soggy meatloaf and weak lemonade. And, as well, my mother's braying cum cries far into the night.

iii

On very hot summer days, I wear a white cowboy hat to keep the scorching sun off my face and neck, and, on very cold winter days and nights, I wear a hood attached to my light blue parka. I've always been partial to hats—and to others who wear hats, women especially—all my life. I look good in hats. I have a good hat head.

iv

My eyes are a delicate light blue. I'm looking at them now, as I write. I've set up a mirror on my desk and I'm looking at my eyes. The mirror shows most of my face, except for what's below my bottom lip, and some of the dark, oblong room behind me. Mostly, I see just the ceiling, which is a dull cream color. When I look in the mirror, I can see insect bodies on the upper side of the rectangular ceiling lamp—little, sharply etched black outlines against the frosted glass. Perhaps, for the sake of my visitors (should they arrive) I'll clean it out.

v

Today, I met a young girl at the tiny village partway up the tall hill. She was golden-haired, eight or nine years old, and she smiled almost constantly.

I encountered her on the porch of the cottage where, only two days ago, I heard an infant crying. I said to her, from the bottom of the porch steps (she was on a small porch swing I hadn't noticed on my other visit), "Hello. Do you live here?"

She smiled with much amusement, as if my question were impossibly stupid, and said, "And where else?"

I shrugged and grinned, embarrassed.

She was wearing a knee-length dark green dress with a white bow at the waist and a fringed white collar. The dress looked a bit dated, though it was clean and seemed well taken care of: "So you live here, in this cottage?" I asked.

She glanced at the cottage's front window, then at me again, nodded, and said, "Yes. And *you* live over *there*." She looked beyond me, at the hill across the lake.

"Yes," I said. "Over there."

"I know that," she said. Her voice was soft, as I'd expected, but she spoke with unmistakable amusement—at what, I had (and have) no idea. "I can see your house," she said, and lifted her chin once, lowered it, lifted it again—a strange, almost mechanical gesture. "If you look closely, you can see it, too." Her eyes sparkled deeply, as if she harbored a secret she had decided to share with no one.

I turned my head, saw only a great mass of pines, then looked at her again and asked, "How do you know where I live?"

She gave me her amused smile, again—such a beautiful, troubled smile—then stood from the porch swing, went to the edge of the porch, put her hands on the railing there, looked straight ahead: "Are you happy?" she said.

"That's a strange question," I said.

"I just want to know if you're happy," she said; she was still looking away, smiling her beautiful and troubled smile.

I said, "Well, who's happy, really?"

"You are," she said.

"Yes," I said. "That's my name, at any rate. Happy."

She nodded, said, "Happy," paused, repeated it, "Happy." She was still smiling, but not in a troubled way, now—more as if she were simply amused. And she was still looking past me, at the tall hill across the lake, where I made my home.

"It's a cumbersome name, isn't it?" I said. "'Happy.'"

She nodded a bit.

"You know what that means, then?" I said. "Cumbersome?"

She stopped smiling, looked at me. "I know this and that," she said. She had green eyes that nearly matched her dark green dress. "This and that, and this and that," she repeated, and looked away again, at my hill. "I know as much as you, Mr. Happy. I know as much as anyone here knows."

"There are others here?" I said.

She cocked her head quickly, another oddly mechanical gesture. "Yes, of course," she said. "There are many others here, in this dull place."

"But I see no one else," I said.

"Neither do I," she said. "Only you, Mr. Happy." Another amused smile, then she cocked her head again. "But that's of no more consequence than a bee dying in a hive." She cocked her head the other way. "I have to go, now," she said.

I heard the cries of an infant from within the house. I said, "Are you babysitting?"

"No," she said.

vi

It's becoming difficult to leave that little village, get into the blue canoe and return to this house, and this room. The village—though all but no one seems to live in it—is appealing, welcoming, even warm (which, at times, I so desperately need), perhaps because it exists, and I know it, because I can prove its existence to my own satisfaction.

If I look very closely, I believe I can see it from my window, though it's all but surrounded by pine forest—I can see a right angle or two, the pitch of a roof.

vii

About fucking:

I have never fucked Epistobel, never fucked any woman, though several have actually asked me to fuck them—"Will you fuck me, Happy? Will you fuck me, Happy?"(Which makes me wonder, *Is she addressing me by name, or asking me to fuck her until she smiles?*).

Let me be clear: I am no Antonio Banderas, but neither am I Quasimodo, nor somewhere in between . I believe that more women look at me than ignore me and, when they look at me, they see something about me that mystifies and, therefore, interests them—the delicate light blue eyes, perhaps, or my gait, which has a sort of purposeful grace, or my apparent distractedness, as if nothing mundane interests me (I like to believe this isn't merely a pose I've cultivated).

Epistobel once said, "You're someone I couldn't avoid." Now, recalling that sentence, I have no idea of its context. It may even have been someone other than Epistobel who said it.

viii

She isn't here, in this house.

The others are. The feral creatures and the always-wild creatures, too.

Sometimes, I hear braying in the middle of the night.

Sometimes, I look out my window at the meager lawn and I see what might be people there, staring up at me. I look at them only for a moment, then I sit down again and do my work.

It has engaged me for years.

I'd be lost without it.

ix

Another thing I do when I'm alone is study my hands very closely. I think hands are miraculous and magical. I've asked myself hundreds of times, *Why do we have four fingers, only?* Obviously, more fingers would be quite useful. Six fingers (with thumb), for instance. Or seven. Admittedly, the brain might have trouble controlling ten or twelve fingers on one hand (twenty or twenty-four on two): the flow of electrical impulses back and forth from the brain to the hands would probably multiply exponentially, leaving our brains with only our hands to think about (meaning, what would our feet and hearts and lungs and eyes do?). But, still, another digit or two or three might be in the cards for us humans at some point in our evolution. Keep an eye on that possibility. And on your hands.

x

I've been thinking about the young girl I discovered in the small village partway up the tall hill and I've come to the conclusion that she was simply someone from *the-town-named-after-the-lake* and that she was having fun with me. Who else could she have been? There's no one in that village but the infant, and even she (or he) could be an imagining, some trick of lesser creatures, or greater, some imperfection of balance, some predilection of wind.

xi

I'm listening to Yo-Yo Ma and he's fantastic. Such focus, which is really what genius is all about—focus. Those of us who aren't Yo-Yo Ma or Einstein or Galileo or Leonardo DaVinci or Thomas Edison or Madame Curie or Beethoven or Bernstein or Hemingway, those of us, in other words, from whom the world will hear no more than hastily written letters and chatty phone calls to friends and relatives, those of us who will be shuffled into our graves with minimal pageantry—go about our lives with our focus divided between the two extremes of the barely necessary and the necessary-in-order-to-survive. And you see, geniuses— those, in other words, who *produce* works of genius (the only true criterion for genius)—may not care a whole hell of a lot about either extreme. They may care about eating and fucking and shelter, but not about the *subtleties* of eating and fucking and shelter. And so what happens to them? They live for *focus*, for the world as a painting or a play or a photograph, a symphony, a light bulb that lights and a phonograph that actually plays music. And when they're dead, we remember their names and their work for quite a long time, but they're still dead, as we are. Still dead.

I believe that many are dead.

The heaps of ashes that knock at my door and stand on the meager lawn below my window, for instance, are dead, as ashes need to be.

And the pretty young thing who brings my meals and slips quietly away.

The tall fourteen-year-old with startling green eyes who made me bleed all over her.

The braying cum-cries of absent moms. Oh, God, the awful braying cum-cries of absent moms!

I don't need any of this!

I must have my work and my focus, my genius, which is what I do and what I am when I'm alone, which seems often, perhaps more than that:

When I'm alone, I do this:

I insert colons. Think of the genius of the inserted colon. The break, the long pause, different from a period, though not startlingly different.

Some of us who may have become non-corporeal are well past being startled even by the sudden hooting of an owl on cool autumn nights drifting inexorably toward summer and some more spacious atmosphere.

The galaxy in Andromeda, for instance.

xii

A dog came in. Small dog with a stubby tail and short brown fur. He had a face as appealing as a soft, cool rain, and so I reached for him and he ran off.

I went to my door, leaned out, into the hallway, looked right, left, saw nothing.

I recognized him, I think. He looked a lot like Bob, who—like many geniuses—is dead.

xiii

Bob was my only dog when I was growing up. I loved him and the rest of the family didn't. They hated him. No one ever said why. When my sister saw him, she muttered, "Fucking dog," and when my father saw him he shook his head and said, "I'd like to know what the hell he's doing here." I don't remember asking anyone in the family why they hated him. I'm sure I did ask, and I'm sure I got unsatisfactory answers, like, "Well, that should be obvious, Happy," or, "Good God, just *look* at him." Such unsatisfactory answers were, I think, common when I was growing up, when I'd ask questions. But I really don't remember any questions or answers. I can only guess.

Which is all right, now. Guessing at the past. It's all right because we can't live there, in the past (or, in fact, we shouldn't), so it's okay to make up various realities for it. For instance, *Martin Luther King became president*, or *The transistor was never invented*, or *Everyone we loved deeply, then, is alive today and we're all happy as clams.*

But who can really judge the happiness of clams, or the popularity of hotcakes, the purity of snow.

She was no virgin when I got hold of her, I'll tell you that!

xiv

I have a deep blue glass out of which I drink water, Pepsi, and cranberry juice, my favorite drinks. When I'm drinking the last bit of liquid from this glass, I enjoy looking about—at this room, or out my one window—through the filter of the deep blue glass. Not only is the room, or the view out my window, suddenly deep blue, it's also convex, and a little concave, too. It's a joyful, if necessarily short-lived, experience. When I'm doing this, when I'm looking through that glass, am I experiencing an alternate reality?

xv

I drove a car here, to this house. It was a Chevy Caprice as big as a tidal wave, and I loved it, so comfortable, rode as if it were on ice. I miss that car.

It was six or sixteen years ago that I parked it. Left it. Came here. And I've been doing my work ever since.

five

"FIVE," I see there. Part of my work. "FIVE." Recollecting. Reordering. Deconstructing and/or re-constructing. Rendering and refutation. Oh the terrible drudgery of it: *(insertion of colon)* Like hauling ashes to Newcastle, as it were.

Bob returned briefly. *The-dog-who-would-have-been-Bob-had-he-been-Bob*, I mean. And he stood as still as stone in my doorway and stared at me as I worked. (Have you been to a pet cemetery? Saddest places on earth. Small stone dogs and smaller stone cats caught in a pose of eternal cute.)

I did not turn to stare back at him. I turned only long enough to note his presence, which seemed to satisfy him, then I let him cloud my peripheral vision and I did my work.

Oh, the terrible drudgery of it.

I would ask myself why I do it if I did not need it so much and if I did not find it so utterly useful. The insertion of colons is only a small part of it: there are other parts, very important parts, *more* important parts which will surface later—the distribution of lists, for instance, which gratifies and soothes me, plus the notation of visual and inexorable decay, which has yet to be explained (though an explanation is promised and forthcoming). As well, I'm looking forward to parenthetical advancement (yet to be explained) and "the teacup metaphor": who knows about that one? It sounds alarming.

ii

And then he was off, *The-dog-who-would-have-been-Bob-had-he-been-Bob*. I went to the door, leaned out, into the hallway, looked right and left, saw nothing but still air and stone trees, called to him, "Bob, oh Bob!" but he stayed wherever he'd gone, and I went to the blue canoe and paddled to the other side of the lake.

Dear Son,

There are Times in Our Lives (some of us, not all of us) when Our memories (the things we actually remember) become unreliable, when they assume multiple, disparate forms, and when they do (and they do because, I think, we age beyond the years [beyond the time] nature granted us at our birth [some of us, not all of us]) these memories stop becoming enjoyable, or worthy, and become (at last) confusing, frustrating, even nightmarish.

All my love,

He did not sign it.

iii

And now, no worse for wear, I have returned. The palms of my hands are a bit worn and red from gripping the oars, but I have artifacts of my trip. They're displayed on my desk and on my windowsill. An orange rock of indeterminate age, for instance. Two white buttons. A dapper shoe (which, I'm sorry, I left where it lay : who wants to carry such a thing?). A glass edge.

Artifacts are very important, don't you agree? They give us a place in time and a place in our own history. They give us something to touch and handle and breathe of, smell and taste. They give us something to believe in, too: and I think we can all believe in artifacts. No one worries about them or attributes them to faith. They're deeply personal, like blood and saliva. Bile, as well. They cannot be refuted.

It's so good and necessary to *believe*. Existence, on any level, becomes tolerable, then.

I think the others in this house are non-believers. They'd have to be. What choice do they have?

iv

I did not see the young girl there, in the village; I saw a somewhat older girl who could easily have been the sister of the girl I first encountered. This somewhat older girl was not as friendly as the other girl; she barely smiled and when she spoke, she looked away, as if she were being evasive.

I asked her name, but she refused to tell me. "Oh my," she said, "what are names?"

And I said, "Names are what they are."

"Piffle," she said.

I have heard few others use that word—"piffle." It's an interesting word, archaic, full of a wry amusement. She used it not as easily as others I've heard use it—Epistobel, for instance— perhaps because it was new to her and she was just trying it out.

⚷

v

When I dwell on it, I'd have to correct myself and tell you that Epistobel never used the word "piffle." Not once in all the years we were more or less together. I doubt she even knew the word.

Memories fade. I must protect my orgasm.

vi

I knew a man who collected soup can labels because, he said, they were facts. *Ingredients: This and that and this and that and this and that.* Just facts. Real things. No fictional encumbrances. No, *This and that and this and that and Harry the Mighty Swordsman and Langley the Hopping Bastard of McFeerson County and this and also that and The First of Four Thousand Years of Beauty and The Weight of Knives in a Cantilever.*

I would like to say that man was my father: That man was my father, whose name was Wilson.

He taught me much, it's true—how to avoid marrying or going out with the wrong woman. How to hammer a nail ("Let the hammer do the work, Happy." . . . "Don't choke up on the handle. Let the hammer do the work, Happy." . . . "No, no, no. Not like that. Jesus Christ, give it to me. *I'll* do it!")

This is what he said about Epistobel: "She's a beauty and she'll give you heartache, so have at her."

My mother once said of my father, "He's not a romantic, Happy. But he gives me pleasure, and that's a precious, precious, precious commodity in this dirty world."

She was always talking about "this dirty world." She didn't mean morally or sexually dirty, I think. It was some other meaning, though it eludes me.

So much eludes me.

That's a good thing. Something to be treasured.

"Falcon. Auburn, Maine"—the name and address of the company that manufactured a stout yardstick I use in my painting. "Falcon. Auburn Maine." Also, "Made in USA."

The shadows of clouds move across the hill at the other side of the lake. Sunshine, blue sky, clouds, some wind, leaves scrabbling across the porch roof just outside my window.

"Oh, you haven't eaten, I see," said the comely young thing not too long ago.

I looked at all of her. "You're consumable," I said, and smiled in a way I hoped she couldn't read (as a flirtatious smile, or a charming smile, or a smile of amusement, but a cryptic smile, one she would remember throughout her days, one she might share with her children, her grandchildren, and so on—one she might look back on as an interesting, retrievable moment in her life).

"I'm not sure I know what you mean," she said, took my tray (ham with mustard and mayo on sourdough, potato chips, a cup of applesauce, tomato juice) and left the room before I could answer.

This is what I would have said had she stayed: "Consumable, meaning digestible. You are consumable and digestible."

A memory worth keeping:

I'm eight years old and I'm a skinny thing, but pretty, with wild blond hair and to-die-for light blue eyes. I'm with several friends, mostly boys, a few girls (all about the same age, these friends: one, a boy named Langston, is eleven, fat, and not very bright: he enjoys the company of eight-year-olds). We're in a little clump, as if we're getting ready for a huddle, but we're conspiring to sing a nasty song and all of us are grinning with anticipation.

There's no one else around. We're in a big park named "Heckley's Park," after a boy who died decades earlier of a disease none of us knows how to pronounce (it's on a plaque at the entrance to the park) and the day is gray and a bit cool and, though there are normally dozens of families here, on good days, having picnics and throwing Frisbees and trying to keep track of happy Schnauzers and smiling Labrador retrievers, there's no one but us in the park, today, and so we can sing our nasty song.

It's a very nasty song.

Here are the lyrics:

"Penis, wiener, ding-dong, vagina."

That's it. Those four very nasty words. And when we sing them—which we're about to do—we can taste them, see them become real things in our eight-year-old brains, even though none of us has yet to see both of the two nasty things the lyrics name—a penis *and* a vagina. If we're female, we've seen only a vagina—our own. And if we're male, we've seen only a penis—our own (poor pitiful thing, nearly lost in the cleavage between our closed legs). And they're interesting things, certainly, but not nearly as interesting as the other thing we've never seen—the penis or the vagina. (It's that sort of decade, that sort of long, suffocating moment in American history.)

And we, the several of us in that moment, caught in our early pre-teens, and longing to sing those nasty words, clump together longer than we should, and grin wider than we usually do, and then break free of the clump and present ourselves in inharmonious song to the park and the open sky.

Penis, wiener, ding-dong, vagina.

Penis, wiener, ding-dong, vagina.

Penis, wiener, ding-dong, vagina.

We laugh when it's done, less than a minute later. We look questioningly at one another and we're all still grinning.

Langston says, "What's a penis?"

I enjoyed writing that:

It's a moment from childhood which will never dissipate, as moments from childhood so often do, especially under unavoidable circumstances which cannot coexist with or, indeed, which negate childhood ("childhood": a beginning, a discovery, an awakening: Shit, I'm on to something here and believe I must rethink my idea about "unavoidable circumstances" which "negate childhood." Oh, the mind, the mind at these long, lingering moments of despair and lofty decrepitude!)

I sang it, just now—*"Penis, wiener, ding-dong, vagina!"*—to a spider who'd reappeared on my screen. I got no response. It's all right.

Spiders don't listen. Why should they? I don't think they can hear, in fact. Or perhaps it's snakes that can't hear.

I can hear: my imaginings, all the voices of the dead.

I have a confession: Epistobel is only a melding of beautiful and consumable women from my past and my fantasies—a long and well-sculpted neck, lips always parted a bit (oh, the darkness and invitation), eyes that follow and know and believe, much-more-than-ordinary breasts, a pleasing rump and vagina, good thighs, feet without imperfection.

If I were a real artist, I would have painted her again and again, in different poses and in different guises, in different places. I would have painted her naked in the woods and seated on a toilet and reading and dancing and knocking at my door.

I have seen her, you know, in all these places, and in all these guises—Epistobel on a ladder, Epistobel eating chocolate almond ice cream, Epistobel leaving footprints in the snow, Epistobel lying beneath me, her lips parted.

There she is, now, naked as the page beneath my pen, this woman who could never be, and was.

viii

These are among the last days of the blue canoe. It's getting far too fragile to row across that angry and punishing lake. Its blue skin is as thin as a whisper. It might split and dump me in and I'd be gone.

"What do you think of that?" I asked the comely woman who brings my food.

She cocked her head at me. No more than that. Just cocked her head and left the room. Left me no food, either.

I should complain.

But I'm not growing hungry.

I'm not growing hungry.

viii

Epistobel stands silently beneath my window.

ix

Off to the other side of the lake in the blue canoe, today, to the hamlet or small village that exists there, halfway up the pine-covered hill: it's that time of year, you understand, so I could see smoke rising from several chimneys, even as I approached from a good distance, perhaps a mile, as I looked in the direction of the village from partway across the lake.

No one answered my knock at any door. I had hoped for better.

I had hoped for, *"Hello. Good to see you. Come in. We've waited for you ever so long."*

But such things don't happen in the real world.

I saw only this: a lithe figure moving away from me through the cool forest.

"Hello," I called. And again, "Hello."

But it was too far. Several hundred feet. And a brisk wind had started. What could I do?

So I'm back here, in my room, with my work. Oh the awful drudgery of it.

And the comely young woman has brought me another supper.

And people I have never met call endlessly to me from below my window.

The End

The End

The End

The End

The End

The End

The End

The End

The End

It is not *The End* of course for this story. It is no story. It possesses no villains, no heroes, or anti-heroes, or conflict of any kind, nor resolution.

I mean only to write it—whatever it may be—until I'm satisfied that it's written and I can return to whatever it is I do here, in this house, in this large room, beneath my window.

six

I had an Aunt named Sarah whom I called "Sarah" because she demanded it: "You must call me Sarah, especially when we're alone," she said.

I didn't want to call her "Sarah." I wanted to call her "Aunt Sarah." It was very important to me to call her "Aunt Sarah." I didn't bother to wonder why it was important to me, then, decades ago: I don't think about it, now.

"I'm going to show you something, Happy," she said.

"You are?" I said.

We were alone in the red farmhouse where I lived with my family, and Aunt Sarah (Sarah) was visiting for a week or longer. She liked to drink and smoke and swear, and I thought that was all right. I even thought it was cool.

"Fuck, yes," she said. "I'm going to show you my naked body."

"You are?" I said again.

It was vitally important to me, then, to actually see a naked female body because I had yet to see one, not even in a magazine, and I was, dammit, fifteen years old (and starting to shave, for God's sake! I used a two-bladed razor made by Gillette, in fact. Twenty-nine cents at Powell's Drugstore, on Oak.), but I didn't want Aunt Sarah to show me *her* naked body because, though it was clearly a wonderful body, it was, after all, *hers*, and she was my aunt, my mother's *sister*, for Christ's sake (so, by extension, looking at her body, and liking it, would be very much like looking at my mother's body and liking it, and that prospect made me queasy).

"Would you *like* to see my naked body?" she said.

I shook my head.

"You wouldn't?" she said. She was clearly disappointed.

I said, "Why do you want me to see it, Aunt Sarah?"

She shook her head sternly. She was wearing a dark dress with tiny white flowers on it. She was buxom and curvaceous and my father enjoyed looking at her. "Goddammit, I've told you, Happy," she said, "—you must call me 'Sarah' when we're alone." She looked at me as if she were waiting for me to speak. But I couldn't speak. I was afraid. "Well?" she said.

"Sarah," I whispered.

She nodded, smiled. My father loved to look at her smile. He told her jokes all the time (bad jokes; farmer's-daughter jokes, traveling-salesmen jokes) just so he could see her smile. "There now, that's better, isn't it?" she said. "For both of us."

"For both of us?" I said.

She put her hand on the top button of her dark dress. "You must know, Happy," she said, and looked at her fingers on the top button of her dress, "that many men would pay dearly to see what I'm going to let *you* see for nothing?"

I stayed quiet.

She looked sharply at me. "Goddammit, Happy, are you listening to me?"

I took a deep breath. I was getting an erection. I was sitting in my father's big, deep green Barcalounger and I was wearing baggy jeans, so I thought the erection didn't show. I glanced quickly at it, saw only blue jean, zipper, shadow. (Oh those damned adolescent erections. They were such a chronic annoyance. When you got one, you were certain all eyes were on it.)

Aunt Sarah said, "Good God, you're getting a hard-on already." She grinned, stared at my crotch, unbuttoned the first button of her dark dress.

"A hard-on?" I said.

"A fucking hard-on, Happy," she said. "Surely you've had them more than once." She was still smiling, still looking at my crotch, where my erection was growing. She said, "A fucking Happy hard-on!" and laughed shortly, unbuttoned the next button, then, quickly, the next, so her abundant cleavage showed.

"I don't want to see your body, Aunt Sarah," I whispered. I'd started to sweat. I could smell it.

"Of course you do," she said, and nodded at my erection. "It's as obvious as a snake in the toilet."

I closed my eyes. I was mortified. I tried to will my erection away. I even whispered—so Aunt Sarah couldn't hear me—"Go away, go away, go away!"

iii

Aunt Sarah's dead. She died from eating bad pies when she was 46, which was ten years after she showed me her incredible naked body. The bad pies were blueberry and they were tainted. Tainted blueberries were a problem, then, in that decade. Something to do with abundant pesticides, or pesticides flagrantly mislabeled.

But she died and is buried and her incredible body is well on its way to oblivion and dismay.

iv

Epistobel, who never existed, is, on the other hand, not dead.

In time, the blue canoe will repair itself. I know this as well as I know my excesses, which have been legion. The blue canoe is a living thing. In its way, it breathes, ages, knows many things. It knows about trees and grasses. It knows about the atmosphere, rain and wind, thunder and sleet and fog. And it knows about the constellations that parade across the sky, night and day—Cassiopeia, Andromeda, the Big Dipper.

I said to the comely young woman who tends to some of my needs, "Would you like to go with me somewhere in the blue canoe?"

She smiled in the way she's come to smile at me—as if I offer heartbreaking amusement—and said, "Certainly. Name a day."

"Saturday," I said.

"That's today," she said, as if confused.

The *dog-who-would-have-been-Bob-had-he-been-Bob* raced past the open doorway then and I nodded quickly. "Did you see that?"

The comely young woman glanced at the doorway, then at me again. "No," she said. "What did you see?" She carried a tray with my mid-day meal on it—grilled cheese sandwich on whole wheat, potato chips and a bottle (with paper cup) of *Wisp*, a citrus drink I've grown to enjoy.

I shook my head once and said, "I saw nothing. A dog."

"Oh," she said questioningly, came to me, handed me the tray, and added, "Well, you know, of course, that we have no *dogs* here, at any rate."

I nodded earnestly, said, "But you do, actually."

She nodded, straightened. "Well," she said, "I suppose there have been rumors."

"There are always rumors," I said.

She nodded again. "I think that many of us exist on rumors, don't you?"

It was a remark I hadn't expected from her. "Yes," I said. "And fantasies, as well, which are a kind of rumor."

She leaned over and touched my nose as lightly as a butterfly. I enjoyed her touch. I felt it in my gut and in my crotch and everywhere else that feeling persists. She said, "Fantasies aren't rumors at all, Happy. They're milk and sweet syrup." And she was gone.

vi

At night I can see the blue canoe. It's as small as a firefly, but I know that it *is* the blue canoe.

I've decided to do what I realize isn't smart—one of these nights, I'm going to leave this room, and this house, and make my way through the forest, to the blue canoe, and across the lake, then to the little village or hamlet that exists halfway up the tall hill. I'm going to do this because the people who live there, in that hamlet, will doubtless be asleep and I'll be able to see who they are and what they're about.

I'm going to do this soon. Perhaps tomorrow night. Perhaps the following night.

vii

The others seem agitated. They race by my open door as if they're chasing something or are in a frantic search for something. But when I go to my door and peer out, I see only backs and shoulders, heels and asses.

viii

Bell Laboratories.
Panasonic CD STEREO SYSTEM SC-EN5.
Compliments or Questions, call 1-800-433-2652.
Easles of Sheffield, Since 1779.
www.hallmark.com

ix

I could not race with Daddy. It was not that he was too quick. He was glacially slow, in fact. And it was not that he was a bad loser. He lost all kinds of races all the time and accepted losing with a smile.

x

But Daddies should never lose.

xi

Epistobel told me that.

"Why shouldn't they lose?" I said.

"Because they're first, naturally, and therefore more important," she said. We were in the middle of a vigorously sexual romp.

"How are they first?" I said.

"My father was first," she said.

"This is a hell of a time to be talking about your father," I said.

But it wasn't, really, because we talked about many things while we were in the midst of vigorously sexual romps. One evening, we discussed grass seed as I held myself above her, arms straight, sweat dripping onto her ample breasts: "Are bluegrass seeds blue?" I asked. I think it was an attempt to forestall my orgasm because she hadn't had *her* orgasm.

To that point, her eyes had been closed. They were always closed when she was on the verge of an orgasm, as if she were watching it approach on the inside of her eyelids. Now, her eyes popped open and she said, "Gee, I don't know!" as if my question had been enormously fascinating.

I shook my head. "I don't either," I managed; I was within the first small and very urgent moment of my orgasm, but I was regretting it, for Epistobel's sake.

As it turns out, bluegrass seeds are, indeed, blue—blue-green, actually. I looked it up.

x

Epistobel did exist, of course. And still may. She existed, or still exists, in my dreams or my fantasies, where I spend so many of my precious or possibly endless moments.

Some people exist on fantasies. I'm not one of them. Fantasies do not come with sell-by dates, copyrights, or trademark notices. They cannot be registered or protected. They move about us like wraiths, complete with tell-tale odors and exaggerated body parts. They lick our navels and genitalia and whisper to us from places we can reach only for a moment, or two, or three.

So many such moments in the span of a life.

xi

I've come to like potato chips. It wasn't always so. I hated them when I was a child. They were too much for my mouth, which was sensitive. I couldn't eat whole wheat bread, either. Same reason. Too much for my mouth. Sensitive mouth. Sensitive gums, probably. But now that I'm past adulthood, I love them. With pickle slices, of course. And a bit of cheese. Cheddar or Monterey jack or some other cheese. Usually a yellow cheese, but sometimes a white cheese.

Only yellow cheese is served here. In this house. But there are bags and bags of potato chips. Small bags. Enough to hold perhaps a dozen potato chips only.

I ask for two bags of potato chips, usually. I write "Two bags, please!" on my lunch order. And I usually get them. Two bags. Perhaps 15 to 20 chips per bag.

My mouth was too sensitive even for Epistobel's breasts when she and I were in the midst of vigorous sexual romping. When she pushed an ample breast into my sensitive mouth I'd usually demur: I'd say, "Oh, I can't, you know," and, because I'd responded that way so often, she'd say, with a little smile, "Yes, I know. But I do love it so—pushing my ample breast into your mouth."

But my mouth isn't quite so sensitive, now. It's not a sensitive mouth. It's an old mouth, and it doesn't produce saliva the way it used to. It doesn't taste food the way it used to, either.

But I love potato chips, at last.

And Epistobel's ample breasts would be such a warm and welcome mouthful, now.

And so.

I am off to the blue canoe.

xi

Lost my way.

xii

Nothing—not unrequited love, a vending machine that will not vend, a car that will not start (or shut off), a fly that will not leave the room, no matter how desperately you chase after it—is quite so frustrating as losing one's way. It shouts of impending old age, faculties not easily alerted or summoned, memories sparked incorrectly or at harsh angles in the synapses—"blue canoe" becomes "boo hoo hoo": *(insertion of colon)* proper names become adverbs: a quote from Descartes becomes a quote from Mark Twain: the lyrics accompanying a Dairy Queen commercial get stuck in the head day and night, making one's dreams cold and tasty, but not easily recollected.

The *dog-who-would-have-been-Bob-had-he-been-Bob* becomes merely a dog who appears at odd times in the doorway.

Epistobel becomes a phantom.

The comely young thing brought lunch and I ate it hungrily, masticated it, am now in the process—I firmly believe—of digesting it.

The gut squeals.

The clock chimes.

xiii

A murder happened in the little house next door to where I lived as a child and it was never solved. To this day I don't believe it's been solved. It involved kitchen utensils, a man named Dave, and a woman named Irene, Dave's lover.

He lived alone and Irene visited him often, though almost always late at night, as if their relationship needed to be hidden. But Dave had never been married (as I recall), and Irene was divorced, so why they chose to carry on their relationship late at night and into the wee hours was something neither my mother, nor my father, nor the neighbors, nor my sister and brother, nor I could understand.

My mother talked about it constantly. She said it was "a mystery," and added that Dave did not seem the type to "carry on with a divorcee so blatantly," which was odd because she'd never even spoken to him, other than to say "Hello," "Good morning" and "Good afternoon."

But she was like that.

She never wrote letters, except when they were necessary.

She never wrote a letter to me.

Though I recall this one, which I reproduce here:

"Dear little Happy," she began (the garlands dangling from the pines are like those which hang sullenly from live oaks):

"Dear Little Happy," she wrote, in spiky, elaborate hand-writing only she could read, and I, too, and my father, I believe, whose name was Wilson, as in Wilson Sporting Goods, makers of soccer balls: "Dear Little Happy," she wrote.

"Dear Little Happy,

Mothers breeze by and through us all, wouldn't you say. Fondly."

She was fond, I think, of short letters. Letters without colons. She wrote many letters, though only when she felt the need. She had a consumable body, as well, like the comely young thing, and like Epistobel, and like my Aunt Sarah, who gave me multiple cold sores, and like the translucent women draped all over the pages of dirty magazines.

Some of them come here and lean over and whisper to me.

☗━┭

A wind brushes past.

I am able, at last, able to part my lips in the expectation of a kiss.

six (again)

Which has played a major role in my life. "Six." "6." One of six children, married six times, father dead at 66, little sister dead at six, six toes on my right foot (the sixth, to the right of my small toe, is barely visible, but is, according to surgeons who elected not to remove it, "a genuine digit."), born in the sixth month (eighth day), in the sixth year (of, admittedly, a fifth decade), have, I believe, an enormously well-developed sixth sense, bear six visible scars on my left hand (four on my right), am nearly six feet tall, and I made the honor roll only in sixth grade, after which I became lazy and disenchanted. Wrote bad poetry in place of listening. And also wandered the empty hallways at mid-morning, wondering what excuse I would devise for missing classes.

ii

But who's to make what of a late-night love affair that ends in murder?

My mother acted mortified, humiliated, aghast, as if the murder had something, after all, to do with her. (And she had always been so fond of saying, "Well, you know, Happy, nothing has anything to do with anything, really, but—and this is very odd—everything has everything to do with everything.")

My father merely raised an eyebrow and his shoulders at the same time—in a shrug—and said, "Well, I don't know."

My brother (Lewis) and sister (Ida) thought the murder was cool. They said, "That's cool!" more times than I could count. ("Jeez, she was really murdered? Do you mean it? You mean, with a knife or something? Jeez! I mean, how cool is that!") I got sick of it. I failed to see what was cool about the murder. It horrified me. I thought the murderer would come after me one night as I slept and I'd simply never awake. (I was as ignorant of Death, then, as anyone on the planet, which would, of course, be *everyone* on the planet [Gosh, perhaps my mother was on to something!]. I vacillated between fear of a constantly frowning, bearded creator in flowing white and blood-red robes who threw down lightning bolts at random, and believing that death was no more than a stopping point for existence, which depressed me so much that, for a while, I kind of preferred believing in the bearded creator in flowing robes who randomly threw down lightning bolts [he did this, of course, to keep his creations in a state of healthy paranoia].)

I shared that fear with my father and he said, "Well, you know, son, that's not really going to happen." (Meaning, the murderer wasn't going to sneak into my bedroom one night and shove a knife into my gut.) "They caught the murderer, I think."

And I shared that fear with my mother, too, who agreed with it and told me to leave my bedroom door locked at all times, even when I wasn't in the room. "You never know what a murderer's going to do, Happy," she said. "He might secrete himself in your closet and wait until you're unawares, then jump out and slice you to bits."

⚍

I asked her about the meaning of "secrete" and "unawares," and she said only, "They're good words. Look them up. Just keep your door locked."

I believed her (Why not? Better safe than sorry.), so I kept my door locked for a year. She liked that, except when she thought I was in my room jacking off, when she yelled through the closed door, "For the sake of Pete, Happy, are you abusing yourself again? Don't you know what trouble that can cause later in life?"

I asked her once what she was talking about—masturbation causing trouble "later in life," and she said, "It's a proven fact, Happy, and can be looked up in any medical journal you'd care to name (I could name none, nor, I think, could she) that self-abuse leads to poor eyesight in middle age and a distinct loss of hearing in the high registers. It also causes excessive flatulation. Especially in the obese."

"Really?" I said. "Is that true?" (Though I didn't know, at the time, what "flatulation" was: I looked it up, found out she meant "flatulence," and I smiled for days.)

"It's as true as yesterday, my boy," she said.

iii

Someone telephoned me. I don't know who. The comely young thing said it was a woman, that she'd asked for me by name—"Could I speak with Happy?"—but that when she—the comely young thing—came to my room to tell me about the call, I was gone. "Where did you go?" she asked, as if concerned.

"I was out," I answered.

"Out? You can't go 'out,' Happy. It isn't done."

"Isn't done?" I said. "Why not. I'm not a prisoner here."

She sighed. "Of course you're not a prisoner. Did I say you were a prisoner? No. I only said it isn't done."

"Going somewhere beyond this house isn't done?"

"Never." She paused very briefly. "Almost never," she added, though not as if she were correcting "never," only modifying it.

"But why?" I said.

"Because no one does it. Never, never. Never."

"No one ever goes anywhere? I don't believe it."

"Well you have to believe it because . . . because you *must* believe it." She paused, glanced about as if looking for more to say, and hurried on, in a voice that was higher pitched than I've come to expect from her, "And if anyone does go out, Happy—if they do go out somewhere, it turns out to be nowhere they really want to be. It's usually some awful place they simply don't want to be, so,*hop-hop-hop*, they're back here as quick as you can say petunia"

" 'Petunia'? " I said.

"A figure of speech," she said. "Petunia. A figure of speech."

"No it isn't a figure of speech," I said. "It's a flower."

"Whatever," she said.

She was being petulant. I didn't like it. Petulance is unattractive in an attractive woman, my father used to say, and I believed him. I still do. I sighed and said, "What did this woman want?"

"What woman?" said the comely young thing.

"This woman who called for me."

"Oh. Yes." She sighed. "She merely asked to speak with you. And she said it in a courteous way, too. There was nothing at all discourteous about her. She had a pleasing voice, I'd say. She said, 'Could I please speak with Happy Farmer.'"

"Oh," I said.

"Yes, well you've been told," she said.

She left a pleasing odor behind as she exited the room. I haven't smelled it on her before. She usually leaves the aggressively artificial odor of Chanel No. 5 (which my father gave to my mother on her birthday and for Christmas and, sometimes, just to give her something: what a sweet man!). This time it was chamomile with a hint of butter and a whisper of vanilla. It didn't seem to be a perfume: I couldn't see a perfume manufacturer actually manufacturing such a perfume—it would merely make people hungry, not libidinous. It's possible the comely young thing had been cooking, though I'm sure that's not one of her duties here.

I enjoyed the smell. I'm enjoying it, now, many hours later. I'm looking forward to her return, even if she's petulant. There's nothing wrong with petulance enveloped in pleasing odors.

iii

It is not good, however, that she believes I simply can't go where I wish to go. It seems to be an assault on my civil liberties or, at least, an assault on my liberties as a spiritual entity (moving about, or wanting to, in the dynamic, albeit static, world of the non-corporeal [which, of course, is a place open to all of us, of any realm, once we realize its existence is a thing of great non-deniability]). It is, after all, assaults on the *spirit* that plague us most in this existence. When we are beseeched to stop masturbating, for instance (as my mother beseeched me *ad nauseum* after my twelfth year), I would say that my very personhood and survival needs (spiritual *and* physical) were being questioned and assaulted. It was, after all, not *her* penis that was being choked.

iv

Epistobel appeared naked in my doorway as I woke from a dreamless sleep. I looked at her for a minute or two, then I said, "Epistobel?"

She turned abruptly to her right and was gone.

She was well-lit, as if my room lights were on: it may be that she was illuminated by the hallway lights and that she wasn't actually standing in my doorway, but back a foot or two from it.

She is always such great consumable joy when she's naked.

As naked, then, as the past.

My gut squeals.

The clock chimes.

The rooster does not crow.

We live in three atmospheres, you know. It's something I learned.

The constellations parade through the heavens. The Big Dipper, Cassiopeia, Orion, The Little Dipper. Stories of bravery and mortality and lust, laid out, even for us, the blind, in the cold sky. They are no more out of reach, to me, than the next moment.

v

This morning, I found that I needed to patch the blue canoe because birds or rodents had made a chestnut-size hole halfway down the port gunwale; it could have been a problem, under some untoward conditions, so I went into *the town named after the lake* and bought a small repair kit. I got a few confused stares from people in the store; not everyone in *the town named after the lake* knows who I am and what I'm doing: today, a rotund man in his thirties, who smelled of gasoline and donuts, smiled at me and said, "Patchin' your boat?" I said yes, and he merely nodded and walked away. He was wearing a hunter's ID tag.

I also bought an ice cream cone at an ice cream parlor in town; the parlor will be closing for the season in a week and I was glad I got there while it was still open. I love ice cream. Chocolate is my favorite I eat ice cream cones often. I like soft ice cream best; it allows for a better lick.

I ate my ice cream cone on a small green bench that sat by a stream not far from the ice cream parlor (its name is "Jeanette's

Ices and Creams," which I find charming). While I sat and ate my ice cream cone, a chipmunk ran across my foot, which caused me to throw my arms out in surprise, which made the ice cream in my cone fly out of the cone and into the small stream—*"Plah!"*

I was unhappy, but I didn't replace the cone. There's magic in the first cone, no magic in replacements.

xi

It was Dave who did the murder. He killed Irene in a lover's quiet rage. Got a dinner fork and plunged it deep into her soft, pale throat. She died slowly, in agony, while he watched, a lustful and quivering grin on his mouth.

Why do men murder this way?

xii

I went nowhere in the blue canoe today. I patched the port gunwale and looked at the patch for a while, until I found it pleasing, then came back here, to this oblong room, and these absent and curious people.

They come and go beyond my open doorway like passersby on a dark street. Sometimes I think I may simply be part of a window display in a strip mall—to the left (or right) a tall cherry dresser, some nondescript abstract paintings on the wall, two small bedside tables with lamps, a mannequin lying prone in bed, mouth open slightly, eyes half closed, as if he's dreaming, or waking. *"With an UltraRest Mattress,"* says a banner above the bed in red, *"you need never worry again about the illusion of sleep."*

Makes me laugh.

NOTHING WILL SURVIVE THE INEVITABLE DISSOLUTION OF SUBATOMIC STRUCTURES.

And that makes me sad.

One-hundred-billion years from now, subatomic structures, composed of subatomic particles, will have joined atomic structures and atomic particles in non-existence and the universe will cease to be. Kittens and parakeets and overweight mothers and little men in gray shortie-shorts and stars and nebulae and great galactic clusters all will have ceased to exist billions of years earlier, leaving only subatomic structures, which will, one by one, and trillions by trillions, wink out of existence.

Goodbye Grandma. Goodbye Snarkie and the lovelorn and the frisky winds that flow from the east, goodbye Mr. Haberdasher and Mrs. Toastmaster and the loons that make a melancholy noise on calm lakes. Goodbye. Goodbye.

Only Epistobel will exist then, because—it hardly needs to be said—she never existed anyway.

It will be a nonexistent universe composed of the formerly nonexistent.

What a concept!

xii

In *the town named after the lake* I saw a well-dressed man attack a stack of pancakes as if it were an accounting sheet. Before pouring syrup on his pancakes (there were five), he cut the stack into four horizontal slices, followed that with four lateral slices, then made four vertical slices (if, indeed, the words "horizontal," "vertical" and "lateral" can apply here, in this narrative, although, for the sake of the narrative itself, they must). After he'd done this, he studied the meager slices for a moment, smiled wanly at his companion—a buxom middle-age woman wearing a short gray skirt and white blouse—who was looking at him with her head cocked a bit and, I believe, a long-suffering grin on her very red lips, as if she had seen him do the very same thing with other foods—then, with incredible care, poured the syrup onto the meager slices as if the whole process equaled major surgery.

I thought, "I don't want to know this man." I thought, "He's not like me." I considered for a moment and thought, "He's not like me, so I don't want to know him." It was a revelation. I had never before realized I was so close-minded. It took me aback; I didn't know what to do with it—that revelation—so I got out of my chair, where my own breakfast of scrambled eggs, toast and orange marmalade waited, went over to the well-dressed, pancake-eating man and introduced myself. Held out my hand.

He didn't take it. He looked at me as if I smelled bad.

His buxom, white-legged companion said, "What are you doing?"

I announced that I was introducing myself, and gave her my name.

"That's not your name," she said, and pursed her lips, as if she were scolding me.

I said, "It is my name, honestly."

She shook her head. "No. It isn't," she said. "It's the name of a children's book."

The pancake-eating man said to the buxom woman, "Is it?" and she said to him, "Yes. I read it as a child." She looked sternly at me. "My mother read it to me, actually. Once or twice a week."

"I believe you," I said.

The pancake-eating man said to me, "What are you doing here?"

I said, "Do you mean—what am I doing at your table?"

"Of course," said the buxom woman.

"I'm trying to introduce myself," I said.

She shook her head again. "Not with a name like that. What sort of parents would give their child such a name? Crazy parents, that's who."

I nodded a little, perhaps in agreement, said, "Enjoy your breakfast," paused, added, "Thank you," and quickly returned to my table.

The pancake-eater and the buxom woman watched closely while I finished my breakfast. They continued watching me as I left the restaurant.

I felt as if I had made a foolish decision in introducing myself to the pancake-eater. I think, now, that I shall not return to that restaurant, ever.

It's called, "Donna's Eats and Hots," and it's blue and white and green.

xiii

Inevitably, there is the little village or hamlet at the middle of the tall hill to deal with: "to deal with" means to consider, to think about, to visit again and explore, to make judgments about—all the processes involved in knowing a place (or person).

The comely young thing said, "You might have told someone where you were going, Happy."

"But I didn't," I said.

It seemed to satisfy her.

I like satisfying her.

x

I satisfied Epistobel now and again. I satisfied her well and with energy. She satisfied me as much, and in nearly the same way. We satisfied each other. It was such a wonderful coming together. So life-affirming. All those very articulate grunts and groans; we are such civilized beasts. Makes me smile a broad and articulate smile. Makes me grunt here, in this dark and oblong room. Makes me wonder who hears it—that grunt, that articulation. *Grunt-a-*

grunt, Grunt-a-grunt! Makes me smile like a fool. I could grunt and smile well into the New Year. I could grunt and smile while the unstoppable constellations parade through my sky.

xi

Well, you know, I'm not in the habit of using such phrases ("life-affirming"). They're trite, even maudlin, even sentimental and meaningless, and I don't know why I used that one, above: I shall not use such a phrase as that again, even when I'm writing about Epistobel's life-affirming orgasms (in a roundabout way), and my own, and our shared orgasms, our "coming together" (you realize).

I do not relish serving up literary bonbons, little word cakes. Makes me smile.

Chime, chime.

xii

I saw Dave running from Irene's house on the night she died. I saw him enter her house and, a half hour or an hour later (Who can be certain after so many decades?) saw him leave, at an odd sort of stilted run (as if his joints had partially merged) from her house. He may even have been making a noise—perhaps some kind of "Whoop!" or cry ("Eeeyiah!"), or he may simply have been weeping so loudly I heard him above the hard rain.

Because, you understand, a pitiless hard rain fell that night. Hard and monotonous (such rains are measurably weaker today, in all parts of the planet, due to the slow but unstoppable dissolution of subatomic structures).

I opened my window as I watched Dave run and weep or whoop (or whatever in the hell he may have been doing) and I thought of calling to him, "Why are you running?" But I kept silence. I watched him run and disappear into the night and the rain. And the next morning, when I woke, I saw that there were police cars around Irene's house and men walking about on the lawn, and in and out of the house, all looking as if they had some grim duty to perform.

Then I saw Irene being taken from the house in a black body bag (which, at the time, I would not have called "a black body bag"). And I ran into the living room—where my mother and father always enjoyed their morning coffee, eggs, donuts and tomato juice—and I said, "I think someone's dead at Irene's house." And my mother looked pityingly at me and said, "Yes, well I'm sure you're right, Happy."

And my father said, "It's Irene herself who's dead," and smiled oddly, as if at some moment of pain that he found pleasurable. "Slit across her neck, you know, Happy. A horrid thing." He was still smiling.

And my mother touched my hand very lightly and said, "Which is not to say that it's something you should even look at, Happy."

"If you look at it," my father said, "then you might be permanently scarred. It might decelerate your growth or cause you to harvest nightmares."

"Yes, certainly," said my mother, and reached out, as if to touch me again, though she withdrew her hand at the last moment. "Harvest nightmares," she said. "Such a civilized phrase. I think it's a phrase you should take much to heart, Happy. Do you understand?"

I looked at her face—which was smiling and earnest and instructive all at once—and then at my father's face—which was also smiling (though still in that odd way) and earnest and instructive, and I said yes, I indeed did understand, to which they both nodded, then I went back to my room, looked at Irene's house, and saw that all was well.

xiii

In a universe that's moving toward dissolution, all the great untidiness to which each of us is exposed during our formative years does, indeed, tend slowly, but implacably, toward the well.

epistobel and the end of nightmares

The village or small hamlet at the center of the tall hill across the lake is lit at night by yellow lights. I can see them from my window. These lights do not move or twinkle and perhaps that sounds cold: twinkling lights are always warm and inviting. But these steady lights invite me.

The comely young thing—whose name I must learn eventually—came into my room and said, "What are you looking at, Happy?"

I turned my head, looked at her: she was framed in the doorway and, because the front half of my room was in darkness, I could see only her silhouette. I said, "I'm looking at the night."

She nodded.

I said, "That doesn't sound strange, does it?"

She shook her head. "Everyone looks at the night," she said. "It's like looking into a mind—one's own mind, perhaps." She stepped forward, stopped. "Are you okay, Happy? Do you need anything? Would you like some refreshment? Would you like some magazines?"

"I have magazines," I said.

She nodded again and came forward another step or two, so half her face was lit by the poor light around me. At times, she's quite striking. In that poor light, for instance. "People need you, Happy," she said (though, at that moment, I could very well have heard it in past tense—"People needed you, Happy."—which would, of course, have been foolish. If people need other people, how can they stop needing them, even if their needs have been met? Needs, like people themselves, transform, change, modify, post-exist. Oh, it's as obvious as yesterday.)

I turned my head, looked at the soft, steady yellow lights halfway up the tall hill, and said, with my head still turned, "I know."

"Perhaps," she said, "and counter to what I said not too long ago, as I recall, you actually can leave this place."

I hesitated only a moment, surprised, but not wanting to show it, then said, "I know."

"Yes," she said. "Of course you know."

ii

Glaxosmithkline.

Pottery Barn. *Made in China*. 3:10.

® Registered Trademark of / Marque deposee de Kimberly-Clark Corporation

Ceramiche Artistiche Sicilane

All of the real.

Good good good to the touch.

In some things, the memory serves with uncanny excellence.

iii

As I recall, my father, whose name was Liam, was not a bad person. He liked animals and drove well. He advised me on romantic entanglements and it was almost always good advice. He died slowly, over a period of months, in great pain. I care for that memory: I go to it occasionally and relive it. It's necessary because pain is something that cooks the gut, and when the gut is cooking we know we're alive.

I don't remember his (Liam's) last words, though I was at his side to hear them, and I heard them. It's a great and unseemly gap in my memory that I hope to correct at some point. Perhaps through travel.

His name was Liam. It's quite a good name. It has strength and lyricism—as he did, almost.

He stumbled often, though. He had no more grace than a child learning to ride a bicycle. He knew about his awkwardness, however, and it was a point of humor for him and for the rest of us.

President Gerald Ford was very awkward, but he wasn't my father.

Gruen.

Philips 40 Watt 48 inch.

Leaving soon. First, dreaming.

What, I wonder I wonder, does one dream afterward?

xi

"Epistobel" was not her name, which I've told you, though it could have been her name had she been able to choose it. Her name was something less interesting and it was inappropriate to her, much, I think, as naming a lovely ghost after a pet Cockatiel would be.

ix

I watched, of course, as Irene was taken away. I saw little, not even her hand falling out from beneath the blanket that covered her (because, of course, she wasn't covered by a blanket, she was, as I recall now, wrapped in a brown body bag zipped up tightly, no place for hands). I said to my brother, who was watching with me, "She talked to me sometimes."

My brother said, "Yeah, she talked to me, too."

"What did she say?" I asked.

He shrugged. "Just, like, 'Hi.' That's all."

"Yeah," I said, "me too." She was being put into the coroner's wagon when I added, "And she said, once, 'Your father owes me money.'"

My brother looked quizzically at me: "Oh yeah? How much?" I shook my head. "I don't know. She didn't tell me."

"Did you ask her?"

The doors to the coroner's wagon were being closed and I said, "No, I didn't."

"I wonder if he ever paid her," my brother said.

"You mean Dad," I said. "I don't know."

"I'll ask him," my brother said.

The coroner's wagon pulled away from Irene's house.

ix

Dark green Mercury. Loud and powerful engine. Not unlike the Chevy that brought me here.

xi

When you look at nearly bare trees late in autumn and you see a few leaves still hanging on, do you think it's some kind of metaphor? I don't.

The-dog-who-would-have-been-Bob-had-he-been-Bob came to my bed and licked my hand as I slept. It made me pee, which made me smile: *(insertion of colon)* how long has it been since I peed while I slept? Oh, I think it's been a time longer than I can remember, like remembering the eruption of Krakatoa, like remembering Pompeii, like remembering the blood of presidents tossed about in black limousines.

Chiming of the clock.

The ruthless pain of the ruthlessly real—endless hiccups, endless dreams of waking.

I must protect my orgasm.

Grab cock and spin.

ix

Aunt Sarah's body molders now like cheese, is now delightfully consumable in the world of the real.

ix

My father always carried two playing cards in his shirt pocket. An ace of diamonds and a joker. He showed them to me once and I asked why he carried them: "Because it's the yin and the yang," he said.

I told him I didn't understand.

He explained yin and yang.

I said, "So which card is yin and which one's yang?"

He said, "Who knows? And isn't that the whole point, really?"

"What's the whole point?" I said. (I was fifteen, perhaps thirteen, perhaps younger, and I was articulate and curious).

He shrugged, stuffed the cards back into his shirt pocket, and walked away (I believe he stumbled over an ottoman).

I brought that encounter up with Epistobel some time later: "What do you think he was talking about?" I said.

"Well, it's obvious, of course," she said.

I shrugged. "Sure," I said.

"I like your father," she said. "He's charming."

I reminded her that he'd been dead for a decade.

"Really?" she said, and looked puzzled. "He's dead?"

"For a decade," I repeated.

"Hmmmm," she said, and touched her finger to her lips. "He always seemed so alive."

And so it goes.

iv

I want to say that he visits me here and gives me advice about my romantic entanglements.

National Geographic.

Scientific American.

Psychology Today.

American Artist.

Mother Jones.

Country Living.

One of my father's pieces of advice about my romantic entanglements was, "Always be ready with a smile." I've followed that advice with all of my relationships. It seems to have worked. Everybody's happy.

The memory serves with excellence.

v

Today, I went twice to the blue canoe and twice to the little village or hamlet that sits halfway up what the locals refer to as "a mountain" but which is really just a tall hill.

Today, more than yesterday, and many of the days which preceded it, I felt stronger, luckier, healthier, more focused, more within the moment that wants to embrace me and, so, I it. Which means that I did not outrun that moment (and push the coming moment into some place where I can never linger, some alternate place of comfort, some *other* little village or hamlet halfway up some *other* very similar tall hill, beneath some *other* set of constellations).

I found nothing there. In that real village or hamlet. Only the houses. I heard no laughter, saw no wraith moving off into the woods. And that's why I went back twice, because I was hoping for more.

Yes, it looked as if it were abandoned, looked as if it had almost always been abandoned, was, really, some nineteenth-century mining village whose inhabitants, by twos and threes, over the space of a few months or a year, left when the mine slowly dried up.

Many such small towns or hamlets exist.

I said to the comely young thing who brought my dinner, "Do you know about the hamlet halfway up that hill?" and nodded at the window to indicate the tall hill.

She shook her head at once and gave me my tray. "Nothing exists there but trees," she said.

I said nothing.

My dinner was excellent—turkey with mashed potatoes and string beans, and a good, hearty apple cider in a leering Halloween mug.

vi

Irene and I had several conversations (beyond the conversation I detailed to you with my brother, on the day she was carried from her little house in a brown body bag). Irene was a philosopher and a poet and we discussed philosophy and poetry often: she was partial to William Butler Yeats and Eric Hoffer, longshoreman philosopher of the 1960s. I was, then, partial to Rod McKuen and felt, also, that I knew quite a lot about the existentialists, whom I could name.

Irene never offered herself to me. I didn't expect it, though I would have liked it.

vii

Phone rings almost nonstop. I hardly have time to ignore one set of rings before another begins. The comely young thing bursts in every now and then and exhorts me to answer the phone, "For the sake of the others," to which I respond, "What others?" to which she answers, "All of the others, dammit!"

If I had any presence of mind, I'd simply have the phone removed. I could use the payphone in the downstairs foyer, although that would require getting mounds of quarters somewhere.

viii

A few real things:

One window that opens. Another that doesn't. They're kitty-corner to each other. The window that opens faces the lake and the tall hill beyond.

Wide-pine floors, well varnished.

Two cotton blankets. One blue, one yellow.

A mass of spider webs in the upper northwest corner of the room. I've thought of asking that this be removed but the mass hasn't grown, so my guess is it's ancient.

A four-panel, dark oak door with Victorian glass knob mounted on a highly polished, and very ornate, brass plate.

A closet door that doesn't close because the house has settled since the door was installed (I assume).

Real plaster walls. Small cracks in the west and south walls.

A bedside table made of pine and built in the Mission oak style. Attractive but cheap. This is where I often find my mail.

This list is necessarily incomplete.

viii

Not long before she was murdered, Irene showed me this poem she wrote to her lover, Dave:

AFTER A TERSE CONVERSATION

Sometimes I talk with you
and I hear myself talking
and it's not the person I believe
I am
who's talking—it's some other
person, and I want
to chase her away, tell her,
"Get your own voice, this is
my voice you're using: I
need it."

But I don't say
a thing to this person.
I let her talk.
She talks incessantly.
She's always at my ear.

"What do you think?" Irene said.
"It's not a love poem," I said.
"But it is a love poem. In a way," she said.
"In what way?" I said.
"In the way that honesty is love," she said.
   I had little idea what she meant. I thought Rod McKuen's poems were good love poems ("Listen to the Warm," for instance),

but her poem wasn't a love poem, at all. I didn't know what kind of poem it was, but I liked Irene.

ix

I still like her. I like the way she exists in my head and what she says to me from time to time, which will never change. I like her very much. I've even grown to like her poem and, at last, to understand it.

Good poem, Irene, I say to her now.

She doesn't say "Thank you." She can't.

x

Here's the room my father used when he was alive:

Notice the comfy chair and the strange looking bookcase with candle, the floor-standing lamp, the cozy glow of the fireplace. I did not paint my father here because I believe that, if I'd painted him, he'd haunt me.

Which is not to say I believe in ghosts, though I do believe in all that's real.

Grab cock and spin, spin, spin.

xii

Ghosts exist no more than the dead do.

That's something my mother said and I think she was right.

So, it's an empty room I painted. Perhaps it's very like the room in which I write. This room. Fake Mission oak table, soft mattress and cracked, real-plaster walls, one window that opens, two windows to see out of, nowhere to go but into the light (or, *ha!*, the night).

"Go into the light!" cried the psychic in *Poltergeist. "Don't* go into the light!" she cried later.

Oh hell, she's dead now.

xiii

Do I actually go anywhere? I wonder. Do I actually leave this room? Do I actually row across the narrow lake in the blue canoe?

It exists.

I carry part of it with me wherever I go—a blue paint chip, part of the forward port gunwale. It's a small chip, no more than an inch square. It rests in my shirt pocket: *(insertion of colon)* it never leaves that pocket except when I wash the shirt, when I transfer it to the top of the fake Mission oak table. I don't wash the shirt often. I'm afraid for the blue paint chip.

Sometimes I move heavily across the bare wood floors, here, to the door, which is often closed, simply to hear my footfalls.

I'm sure you've done the same thing from time to time—part of that questioning process we all go through when our existence seems out of reach, malleable, as real as the space between stars.

xiv

I've heard of a place in Argentina where people raise spiders for their silk (which, I'm sure you know, is stronger, ounce for ounce, than steel). It's called "The Spider Ranch" and it gives me the willies. Who'd want to live at a spider ranch? Just imagine if there were a spider revolt or a spider strike or something: *"Work stoppage in effect! We want more flies!"*

I heard about The Spider Ranch today during a quick visit to the town named after the lake. I was having a breakfast of coffee, eggs and toast, not enjoying it very much (runny eggs, burnt toast, brown water masquerading as coffee) and I noticed two spiders straight out of a horror show on the outside of the window beside me (which overlooks a parking lot: dozens of pickups and SUVs): "Jesus," I muttered. "Jesus Christ!" I didn't realize the waitress was standing beside my table with a pot of *faux* coffee:

"Jesus Christ, indeed," she said.

I looked quickly at her, startled. "Sorry," I said, because I assumed I'd offended her religious sensibilities.

She smiled. "You know what?" she said. "There's a place in Argentina called 'The Spider Ranch.' They got millions of those awful things." She nodded at the two horror-show spiders on the outside of the window. "They sell the silk. You know—the webs. I guess it's great stuff. Jesus, I think you can build skyscrapers with it, or something." She held up the pot of coffee. "More?"

My Father Was A Very Fastidious Man Who Lived a Scrupulously Clean Life

Often (though usually in the morning) my father came out of the bathroom, looked at us kids and my mother as we sat around the dining room table, and said, "I've experienced an unsuccessful flush." Then he'd nod a little, as if to add some unspoken phrase, and then he'd go into the living room where he liked to sit and listen to the morning news before heading off to work.

We all knew what "an unsuccessful flush" meant; he'd clogged the toilet and we were not allowed to use the bathroom until he'd dealt with it.

I once said to my mother, "I don't care if he clogged the toilet. I just gotta pee." And she said, "I know, dear. But your father would be mortified if you used the toilet just now. Before he's had a chance to make things right."

It was a theme I heard quite a lot in that house. If something went wrong, life all but stopped until it was "made right." If the car wouldn't start, it needed to be fixed ("made right") before anyone could continue living his own life. If a faucet leaked, it needed to be "made right." If one of us was sick, that person needed to be "made right," or life, for the rest of us, simply couldn't go on.

"We, as a family, are part of a sacred whole," my father explained once. "We exist as a physical reality in a desperately spiritual universe: do you understand what I'm saying to you, Happy?"

I shrugged.

He smiled. "You will, I'm sure," he said. "After time has passed and you acquire wisdom."

I shrugged again.

He said, "The acquisition of wisdom, Happy, is the only true purpose of age."

I sighed. I needed to get away from him because he was spouting off again, making me feel stupid (without meaning to), and the day was warm and bright (in an era when I valued such days), and I knew he understood the meaning of a sigh.

"Go ahead, now," he told me, and gestured toward the front door. "The sun needs you."

I think that was the most valuable thing he ever said to me.

xiv

I'm sitting in the blue canoe as I write. I write in a Mead® Cambridge® Limited Business Notebook—1 Subject, 80 Pages, Legal Ruled, 5″ × 8″, Black. Pages are a light green/blue. I write with a white ballpoint pen (Did you know ballpoints weren't invented until the 1950's?) that has the words "20th Century Clocks" imprinted on it in red.

I can fit only 100 words or so on each page because my handwriting is large, with lots of flourishes—very long upstrokes and equally long down-strokes. I've been told my handwriting shows affection. If that's true, I don't care.

I don't row as I write, of course. That would be impossible. As I write, now, the oars are inside the gunwales and I'm moving at a slow walking speed toward the eastern shore of the lake and the tall hill. I'm halfway there. A few other boats share the lake with me this morning, though they're at a distance. One sports two large sails; it's maybe a mile north, near *the town named after the lake* and it's moving almost imperceptibly west: it catches the morning sunlight now and again. Another, a rowboat, is perhaps half a mile northeast of me: I believe there are two people in it, fishing. One of these people is wearing a bright red jacket. I wonder if it scares the fish.

When I look over the starboard side of the canoe, I see Epistobel's face just below the surface of the water.

"Hello," I say to it.

She closes her eyes and goes away.

epistobel and the missed opportunities

If you head east on Routes 5 & 20, and if you keep an eye out for the names of hamlets and small towns, you will eventually come across the place where she was born: it's called Centerville and it consists of two dozen houses, a service station, and a Mom and Pop grocery called "Edwina's Goods and Produce."

Epistobel is buried a quarter mile south of Centerville, in a cemetery which, I believe, has not been cared for since its first inhabitant was interred there.

Her gravestone bears her real name and her date of birth and date of death: *(insertion of colon)* I put red roses on her grave long before I came to this place. When I went back to her graveside some time later, I saw that the roses had dried perfectly, and that they still looked almost fresh. I assumed it was a sign from Epistobel herself, though I couldn't say what it meant: I clung to this belief until her real name vanished from my memory.

I wrote this for her, then:

NOTHING TO FEAR

No alone in this house we share.
We sing to each other without voices.

We move about, in good sight, while the other
sleeps, and we wake
to the other, even at some
improbable distance. We have
our own rooms, certainly—mine is
covered in pages of you, yours in
flowers, verse, your own
music.

We will inhabit this house together
through more time than we may
have. I'll wake you on a
morning when morning is forever,
and offer you toast, tea,
myself. And you'll grin a grin
as huge and appealing as full day,
and accept. Will it matter the distance,
then,
when there is no distance,
and our bodies are the stuff
of nebulae
and memory.

iii

I remember we were haunted in one of our houses. I'm talking about my two sisters and two brothers, my mother and father and I.

We lived in half a dozen states over a period of ten years, in several houses within each state. And, in one of those houses, we were haunted.

I remember little about the house or the haunting. I remember that all of us were alive when it happened and that I was in my early teens, which means it happened when my two brothers were in their mid-teens and my sisters weren't quite ten years old.

And I remember that my father announced the haunting to us one evening at dinner (he announced many things at dinner: in that decade, dinnertime was the very best time for making announcements).

He said, with great seriousness, and after looking earnestly at each of us in turn, "There is, I believe, a specter, perhaps several specters, sharing the house with us."

My brother Tom, five years my senior, said, "What's a specter, Dad?"

My father answered, "Tom, it's a wraith."

I said, "Yeah, I know about wraiths. I read about them in school last week."

"Oh?" said my mother. "Why would you be studying such a subject, Happy?"

Tom said, "I don't know what a wraith is, either, Dad." Tom always admitted ignorance without a trace of self-consciousness. At the time, I thought it was a sign of weakness.

I said to Tom, "It's a ghost, you nitwit."

My mother reached across the table (I always sat across from her) and slapped me in the face, though not hard enough that it hurt. I recoiled as if she'd hit me with a baseball bat.

"Over-reaction, son," my father said, and looked sternly at me. "It's very unseemly in a smart person such as yourself."

I shrugged.

My mother said, leaning over the table so her chest (which was ample) grazed one of two big bowls of mashed potatoes, "You apologize to your brother this instant, Happy, or you'll find yourself with an empty stomach tonight. Do I make myself indelibly clear?" (She never said "absolutely" or "perfectly" clear: it was always "*indelibly* clear," which made a second-hand sort of sense, I guess.)

I shrugged again, looked at Tom, who was smiling at me the way he always smiled, as if all was right with the world, even when it wasn't, and said, "Sorry, Tom."

"For what are you sorry?" my mother demanded.

I looked at her. "For calling him a nitwit," I said.

"Direct your apology to your big brother, please," my mother said, then straightened, saw the mashed potatoes on her chest, pursed her lips, and dabbed with great irritation at the potatoes with her pink and blue napkin.

I looked at Tom and said, "Yeah, well, so I guess you're not a really a nitwit," though I didn't mean it, which I'm sure he understood, and he said, "Okay," still giving me his nitwit smile, and my dad said, "All right, then, that's settled. Perhaps we can get back to the subject at hand."

And my mother said, "We'll not discuss such things in front of the children, Liam," and my father said, "I think it's important, Miriam," and my mother said, "Please consider that these are imaginative children who have yet to gain full expression of their intellects, Liam," and he apparently thought about this a moment because he said, "That's truly an acceptable argument, Miriam."

"I'm glad you agree with me, Liam," my mother said; she was still dabbing at the potatoes. "You never know what this talk of a wraith in the house will do to these boys. They might become so badly agitated and upset that they'll be squirreling into the bed with us in the middle of the blessed night, just as they did when they were younger." She nodded, as if in agreement with herself.

"I think it's cool," I whispered. "I think the ghost is cool. I hope she visits me every night."

With incredible speed, my mother reached across the table and slapped me hard across the face again. "That is a very inappropriate thing to say, Happy. One might think you're talking in a libidinous way. Are you?"

I shrugged. "Libidinous" wasn't a word I'd yet learned.

The wraith in the house was never discussed at dinnertime again.

iv

That's when and where I grew fond of Roman numerals. In that house, because of the wraith who haunted it. She left Roman numerals on the walls in my bedroom and in the cellar, near the furnace. She left them in red, and Tom said, "Gee, that's blood, I think," though I could see that it wasn't blood because blood, when it dries, isn't bright red, which this stuff was, and I said to him, "That's paint, Tom. Dried blood is sort of brown."

He nodded and said, "Like a scab, huh?"

"Yeah, Tom," I said.

And he said, nodding at the Roman numeral on the cellar wall, "What is that? A six?"

I told him it was six, though it was nine.

Rage, Rage against the dying of the light . . .

ix

Graham Nash sings, "I saw the back of your dress/as you slipped through the door/as you slipped through the door." God that makes me sad.

x

Helicopter flies low over the lake, looking, I think, for a drowned person.

xi

So noisy. Upsets the quiet of all things. The quiet of the drowned person, too. "Let me rest," says the drowned person. I hear her. Desperate, quiet voice, trembling just on the edge of speech. But the rotor blades shout "No!" The rotor blades hear nothing. They are real things, like soup, or magnets.

I'm interested in the drowned person. Clearly she went out for breakfast (She told me so; I heard her.), then went out onto the lake in a boat, sated, ready to begin the day. And fell overboard. *Plah!*

It was a woman to whom this happened, as I've told you. She ate a light breakfast, was thinking of eating a light lunch, and a light dinner. She spelled "light" as "lite" when she planned her meals, which made her boyfriend or husband or lover grin, but he kindly said nothing because he or she was a good lover who'd never poke fun at her. Sensitive people. Both of them. The woman and her lover.

And she had, of course, dark hair that fell halfway down her back in soft curls that she almost continuously vowed to cut off because, she said, "they weigh so damned much." Makes me smile.

"And as you sleepily rise," writes Graham Nash, "you'll find I'll be there, you'll find I'll be there."

The helicopter has departed and has apparently found no drowned person.

xii

I stand now at the opposite shore of the lake, my Meade Spiral-bound notebook in hand, and I'm trying to locate the house in which I live and work, but I can't: *(insertion of colon)* there are too many trees, a wealth of pines.

Now (later) halfway through the woods to the little village or hamlet, I've stopped for a rest, and have heard something move swiftly, with urgency, through the tall grasses—something small, nothing that could do harm. A vole, perhaps. Many voles live here, on this tall hill.

And just then, a moment ago, I heard, as well, the voice of a child calling from further up the hill. Young girl's voice, I think. "Who are you?" the voice called.

And I answered, "Happy Farmer. Happy Farmer."

And now, after waiting a full five minutes, I've received no reply, so I'll continue my climb.

xiv

Found blood there, in that village. Rust brown. Dry. Old blood.

xv

The comely young thing came to my room and announced that a body had been found in the lake.

"Who was it?" I asked.

The comely young thing shook her head and scowled. She was clearly frustrated that she knew little about the identity of the person in the lake. "I don't know," she said. "A woman."

"Long dark hair that fell in soft curls halfway down her back?" I said.

She gave me a questioning look, shook her head again. "I don't think so."

"But how would you know?" I said.

She was carrying my dinner on a tray. Mashed potatoes, meat and a green vegetable. She brought it over: "I wouldn't," she said. "That's why I said 'I don't think so.'"

She gave me the tray with my dinner on it, which I took graciously from her.

I enjoyed the sudden appearance of the helicopter yesterday. I enjoyed the noise it made. I enjoyed my conversation with the dead woman, her pleasant voice so filled with desperation and urgency.

xvii

Dear Son,

There are Times in Our Lives (some of us, not all of us) when our memories (the things we actually remember) become unreliable, when they assume multiple, disparate forms, and when they do (and they do because, I think, we age beyond the years [beyond the time] nature granted us at our birth [some of us, not all of us]) these memories stop becoming enjoyable, or worthy, and become (at last) confusing, frustrating, even nightmarish, and so there we are, caught (through happenstance) beyond the age when death should have claimed us, in a hellish stew of memories we may or may not be parent to, and so we search everywhere for a good and proper place to die. What else can we do? What choice do we have? But death has already forsaken us once. Odds are it will forsake us again.

All my love,

He did not sign it. He signed most of his letters, but not that one.

He's a man I much remember, though only in pieces, the way I remember songs and relationships. He used words as if they were glue and hammers.

xiv

Nothing I do makes me believe in God, which is a subject as unimportant to me as daytime TV (I own no TV: I own a Sony, "real oak," tabletop radio, circa 1961).

I can't even write about it (my opinion of God) because this story involves helicopters, body bags, quirky, authoritarian mothers, an anonymous dog and nitwit brothers. God has no place in it. God doesn't even speak to me through Epistobel. And Epistobel doesn't speak to me.

The blood in the village or hamlet halfway up the tall hill across the lake lay in a thin diagonal line across the front porch floor of the little house in which I heard the cries of an infant during an earlier visit. I leaned over to study the articulation of the blood spatters and concluded that the bleeding person had been walking *away* from the house because the blood splatters tended to point in that direction (which, I decided, was northwest, off the porch). I found this very satisfying.

My attempt to follow the line of blood over the ragged grass in front of the house was unsuccessful, so I had no idea where the bleeding person went, though I assumed he or she disappeared into the piney woods that surround the village. I wondered if it could have been the drowned person, but decided almost at once that the idea was foolish.

I knocked on the front door of the little house, got no response, and hollered, "Is someone home?" and, still getting no response, hollered, "This is Happy Farmer. Is anyone at home?" I got no response. I hollered, "If someone has suffered an injury in the house, perhaps I can help."

ii

I got no response.

I came back here, to this house, to this room.

The-dog-who-would-have-been-Bob-had-he-been-Bob galloped past my open door only a few moments ago. He didn't stop to look confusedly at me, as he often does; he seemed to be chasing something. Perhaps a vole. There are many voles in this place.

Did you know that voles are rodents closely related to muskrats and lemmings? It's something I remember.

xv

Here's a painting of what my mother used to drive to work:

She was a teacher. She taught "Early Science" at what would now be called a "middle school" in New Jersey, where we lived for many years. Her name was Cecilia and she was tall, graceful, and quite lovely. She drove the pickup truck (a red 1953 Chevy) to work because it had been her mother's pickup truck and my mother was very family oriented. She said often, "What was good enough for mother is certainly good enough for me."

The pickup truck my mother drove had wheels, of course, but this is the way I remember it after she died at 48 while riding a bicycle to work (the pickup truck wouldn't start that morning) and was hit by a man in a delivery van. The man's name was Stan. He professed great sorrow at hitting my mother. "I didn't see her," he cried. "Christ, I didn't see her!"

After her death, my father had the pickup truck's wheels removed and the body put on cinder blocks in our front yard on a quiet street in Hoboken. It was a sort of shrine to my mother, I think, though the neighbors complained bitterly. A couple of them even drew up a petition, which they presented to the powers that be at the Hoboken City Hall, to have the pickup truck removed from our front yard. Eventually, they won, and the pickup truck was hauled to a junk yard many miles away.

All of what I have just written is breathtaking and true.

xvi

I've often wondered what I would have done had the myth of Epistobel not entered my life—dawdled about, wept long into the night, lived in various northern states, found myself unable to pine? I'm virtually certain much of that might have happened. But she and the myth that surrounds her have kept me living sensibly, which is to say she has kept me living at least a yard or two from emotional anarchy, where I've managed to feed myself and keep a canary-colored roof over my head.

Epistobel once said to me, "I think you're lost, Happy." I asked what she meant and she said, "I think you're looking for something but you don't know what it is." She shrugged. "So you're lost."

I nodded and said I agreed with her, though I was lying: (insertion of colon) I liked to agree with her because it made her agreeable, and when she was agreeable, she offered herself lavishly to me and we would engage in yet another of our vigorous sexual romps.

She said, "I don't think you agree with me, Happy." She smiled. "I think you simply *want* me. I think you simply lust after me."

"There's nothing simpler or more honest than lust," I said.

"So you're not denying it?" she said.

We were in a place that was warm and wet—a combination I usually dislike. I think it was an open-air library.

"I deny nothing," I said with great cavalier detachment (which I'm sure made her passionate, now that I recall it: I've come to learn that women everywhere—even the myth that was Epistobel—are excited by great cavalier detachment. It's incredibly cool. In a strange and oblique way, it speaks of immortality. Scratch that. I'm full of steaming horse shit! This is no way—obfuscating, bending the evidence of an often ludicrous existence, simply so I can protect my orgasm. Orgasms are a dime a dozen. A dime a hundred. At this very moment, there are doubtless a billion orgasms happening on the planet: it's surprising they don't knock the earth off its precarious axis.)

xvii

The helicopters have returned. Three of them. They're very noisy—such a racket. I can't hear my music (Debussy), only the throttling cacophony of the helicopters. Why three? What's the need? One helicopter could easily search for *several* drowned people.

xviii

Moments ago, I asked the comely young thing about the helicopters and she said, "I don't know, but they're certainly noisy, aren't they?"

"It sounds like the race track," I said. "Have you ever been to the race track?"

"I used to go the demolition derby in the town where I grew up," she said.

"Where was that?" I asked.

"Upstate," she said. "Way upstate." She nodded at my tray. "Would you like anything else, Happy?" She smiled graciously, took my tray: I'd eaten most of my dinner, although the canned peaches had an odd metallic flavor. "Why do you use canned peaches?" I asked.

"They're really better for you, Happy," she said.

"I don't think so," I said.

"And they're cheaper," she said.

"I would prefer fresh peaches," I said.

"Yes," she said. "Yes, of course. And why not? Fresh peaches are always preferable." She smiled coquettishly and left the room.

She was wearing a florid perfume—even more artificial smelling than Chanel—and its warm and sexual odors linger.

Epistobel wore no perfume. She was allergic to all perfumes and musks. She broke out in hives simply upon smelling perfume. It was an awful sight. Hives on soft skin. "Oh don't look at me, Happy. I'm so ugly, now!" But I assured her that even Death could have no power over her great beauty, which made her tilt her head and say, "That's very nice, Happy, but it's also a bit creepy, don't you think?" I smiled and said I was sorry, that I wouldn't mention it again, and I often kept my word, which I'm sure she appreciated.

xviii

If I close my eyes and reach into empty air, I can feel the wood that the houses in the little village halfway up the tall hill are made of; (insertion of semicolon) it's old wood, and rough, and it almost hurts the skin. If I were to knock on that wood, the sound would certainly rouse no one, even if I knocked very hard.

In such a universe as that, it's doubtful I can ever be surprised.

But I am surprised. Constantly. Continuously. Like a newborn set down in the middle of an expressway. My world is a place of nebulae, constellations, exploding stars, and lovers I've no doubt simply imagined into existence (to protect my precious orgasm).

Perhaps I came here from the galaxy in Andromeda, perhaps I was sent here by tall, bald aliens to find my doppelganger, because that is what the aliens in Andromeda do. And it is they who have formulated Epistobel out of stuff that exists there—in Andromeda—and they who have formulated the little village or hamlet that lies halfway up the tall hill, they who have formulated *the-dog-who-would-have-been-Bob-had-he-been-Bob*, they who have formulated the comely young thing who doesn't answer my questions (perhaps because I don't formulate them correctly), they who have formulated the blue canoe, my mother's 1953 pickup truck, the quarter-size spiders.

I am *so* bedeviled. I'm like a newborn plopped down in the middle of a busy expressway, fascinated and fearful. What can you do? You're a newborn. You watch the traffic zip by, watch drivers gawk ("Oh my God, what's that? Oh my God, it's a baby!"), hear cars screech to a halt, hear the crunch of fenders, screams, curses, pandemonium, smell blood and gasoline, though you don't know it's blood and gasoline and pandemonium: it's your universe and you can't define it, you can only experience it, because you're a newborn plopped there by tall, bald aliens from the galaxy in Andromeda, and zip, *thunk!*—your time's up.

Who can live in such a universe? Who has a choice?

xviv

First cogent thing I've written in some days. Must be my new diet.

xvv

A woman I knew was always dieting, though she stayed fat. "I don't understand it, Happy," she said. "I'm always dieting, but I stay fat."

"Maybe you eat the wrong foods," I said. I was eighteen years old. I knew nothing much, though I knew some things (for instance, that the kind of food you eat can make you fat).

She said, "But I do. I eat the right kind of foods, Happy. Lettuce and meat."

"Maybe you should exercise," I said.

She had a round, pleasing face that was almost always red (except when she was asleep). Her eyebrows were very dark and her hair wasn't quite as dark. She wore her hair in ringlets, though she was a grown woman. At eighteen, I thought that was odd. She said, "But I walk, Happy. I go to the store once a day. And back again with my groceries."

"That's good exercise," I said, though I didn't remind her that the store she went to was only two doors from her house.

"So you see," she said, "I exercise and I eat the right food, but I'm still fat." She shrugged and held her hands out, as if confused by the entire issue.

Her name was Dolores and she married an attorney who specialized in medical malpractice litigation. His name was Stewart ("Call me Stu.") and he liked to wear brown suits with brown shoes and smoked a big brown cigar. He smelled heavily of cheap deodorant and cigar smoke. When he and Dolores were at social gatherings, he grabbed her ass a lot.

Dolores and Stewart are not among the many people who inhabit this place, and I view that as a plus.

My guess is that at least 18 people inhabit this place with me. Perhaps, at some point, introductions will be made.

xviv

What am I doing here?

xvv

What is anyone doing here?

I asked the comely young thing where she lived. "I live, oh"—she gestured expansively toward the northeast—"over there."

"I don't understand," I said.

"It's not really a town that I live in," she said. "I guess you could say I live in the countryside."

"You live in a house in the country?" I said.

"Well, of course," she said, and gave me a particularly comely smile. She bent over, adjusted my blanket. She was wearing her white blouse unbuttoned to the third button and when she bent over she gave me an astonishing look at her very ample cleavage. "What did you think?" she began. "Did you think I lived in a hole in the forest?"

"Well, I . . ." I began, but didn't finish.

"Of course," she said.

I thought of my Aunt Sarah and her cleavage, which, by now, has turned to cheese.

xivvii

I have received yet another phone call from the person who has called me countless times already. This time, she had a very threatening tone, and she used words and phrases I can only describe as provocative.

xiviiiv

This afternoon, I scratched my arm till it bled. The sight and smell and feel of the warm blood trickling down my arm was comforting, almost reassuring.

The comely young thing came a few steps into the room, then, saw the blood, put her hand to her mouth, and left quickly. She hasn't returned.

xiv

I have decided to go at night to the blue canoe, and then to the village halfway up the hill. I will, perhaps, not do it tonight, or tomorrow night, but on a night of my choosing. Soon, perhaps.

My father once told me, "Always do in the night what can be done in the night, and the day will forgive you."

I told him I had no idea what he was talking about.

He smiled his daddy smile.

xiviivxi

x

Where can you go if you can't go home again? Can you go somewhere that isn't home? And what can you do there? Imagine, remember, regret? We humans do so much of that. If God were an intellectual he'd shoot himself.

This morning I have the first false snowfall beyond my window. It's a false snowfall because it won't last through the afternoon; perhaps it will last only a few hours. It falls almost as if it's reluctant to fall.

"Look at that beautiful snow," I said to the comely young thing, but she had already appeared and disappeared from my doorway, so I found myself talking to no one. It's all right, though. Talking to no one can be fruitful and compelling and, besides, we never really talk to *no one*. There's always someone listening.

xi

I've decided to call *the-dog-who-would-have-been-Bob-had-he-been-Bob* Bob, in honor of my late beagle, Bob.

Bob, formerly *the-dog-who-would-have-been-Bob-had-he-*

been-Bob, isn't the Bob I once knew, of course. We can never replace the dead, whether they're beagle or human. But we can honor them through the respectful re-use of their names.

And so, I shall call *the-dog-who-would-have-been-Bob-had-he-been-Bob* Bob, and I shall call the comely young thing whose visits seem to be growing less and less frequent "Epistobel," though she hardly compares or measures up to the real Epistobel who was, after all, not Epistobel, either.

Note this: It is excruciatingly hard work designing a universe to dwell in and be made happy by.

xii

I can hardly do it alone.

xiii

But, as it turns out, there is no other way to do it. It's what I have been bequeathed by the existence I've morphed into. *Faux* coffee and burnt toast. A bit of moldy marmalade. Scrumptious aunties willing to expose themselves for their own convenience. Fathers who devised more faces than Picasso.

Remember *Guernica*? All that anguish? I have had no anguish whatever compared to that. I have had golden days and memorable nights compared to that.

But I wasn't there, in Guernica. And neither were you.

And so to sleep.

xiv

New voice, new person: I am Epistobel and I'm wishing Happy Farmer a restful evening which will lead to a successful morning.

He sleeps deeply, does not move about. He sleeps on his right shoulder through the night. I've seen it. He snores a little, though it's not an unnerving or enervating snore. It's like the sound of a bullfrog deep in a swamp. It resonates and echoes. It even brings pleasure. I've never told him this, however, though I suppose I'm telling him, now.

I am a night person. You could say that I exist at no other time than the night, but you'd be wrong.

xv

(Insertion of italics.) Piffle! I have no idea who wrote that up there, that paragraph, though I realize it could have been any of a number of people who exist in this place with me, who have their own rooms, certainly, but don't give a good goddamn about violating the privacy of others!

I am very bothered, irked, by the idea that whoever wrote that paragraph has read the rest of this narrative and may think I'm a loon, which I am not, and may go off to the authorities and report me, which will lead to my removal from this house, which would make it impossible for me to use the blue canoe.

The whole matter is urgent and requires MUCH thought.

8:00 PM of the following day

I feel it is I who wrote that paragraph.

chapter one

She did not recognize the middle-age man who came with a broad and intrusive smile to her door. He was tall and clean-shaven and his eyes were nearly blue, with a hint of gray, and the first words out of his mouth when she opened her door were, "I've been on a very long trip, but now I've returned. Hello."

She couldn't help grinning at him. He seemed so earnest, like a puppy. But she forced herself to stop grinning and said, "I'm afraid I don't know you, sir."

He cocked his head (as a puppy does) and said, "Aren't you _____" and used a name which she didn't recognize.

She said, "No, I'm not."

He cocked his head the other way.

The day was blue and green and startling, just the kind of day she enjoyed, and she wasn't at all sure that the middle-age man at her door was having a negative or a positive impact on her enjoyment of it.

She realized, suddenly, that she was naked.

xiivii

Today, I floated in the blue canoe for hours. The bright late morning became afternoon, the afternoon became dim early evening—

when the dim constellations start their nightly parade across the sky—and I made my way back to this house, to this room.

I was peppered with questions as I came in:

"Why have you returned, Happy?" and, "Do you think we were lonely without you?" and, "Do you know that Epistobel is angry? Do you know she had your dinner for you but there was no one around to whom she might serve it?" and "Where were you, Happy?" and, "Does it make you happy to be away from this house?"

I ignored these questions and took the stairs straight here, to this room.

No one was waiting for me.

My cold dinner sat in a green plate on a blond tray—turkey slices, mashed potatoes, a chef's salad, fresh mango, and a whipped cream surprise, which had melted and which, anyway, smelled like bologna.

I write and write and write, which is my work, and it is all to a purpose. If I don't write, how can I know anything?

iixiv

chapter two

Surely it had only been a dream, he told himself. Surely the woman he had known as his lover hadn't answered her door naked and, as well, professing to know nothing of him.

Surely she had merely been joking, as was her habit, which he adored. How right and fair it is to love even the odd or annoying habits of one who is loved.

But now she lived in that dingy house, under dingy circumstances, under the threat of hypothermia these cold, cold nights, and she moved through her daylight hours beyond windows which were nearly opaque.

What could he do for her but love her? What did she demand of him?

Surely he needed to take these questions to people who knew better than he about everything.

Dr. Amelia Pancake, for instance (who shared her last name with several of the near-famous, now dead), whom he had been seeing professionally for more than several years and who dealt with him as if he were actually lucid in a world filled with nothing but noise.

"Well," said Amelia Pancake, "it's a quandary."

"No," he said. "It's a conundrum."

"Quandary, conundrum," she said. "I doubt it really matters."

"Definitions matter a lot," he said.

"There are few precise definitions in this anarchic world," she said.

He looked questioningly at her. She was round, cherubic, had shoulder-length dark hair that she wore in ringlets, as if she were an eight-year-old. Her teeth were very white but crooked, doubtlessly, he thought, from the effects of bad braces, and her mouth was preternaturally large, though her lips were as thin as spaghetti. She said, "You can't even define *her*, or yourself." She gave a moment to silence, then added, "There are no precise definitions, Mr. Grimm."

His name was Andrew Grimm. He'd been told to change it. "No one wants to be walking around in a store and hear, 'Paging Mr. Grimm,'" a close friend once told him. "People will think that Death himself is being paged." But he had kept his name because he liked it; people often asked him if he were related to the Brothers Grimm, who wrote so many grim fairy tales, and he always said, "I believe that I may be, but it's a subject I've yet to research."

He said to Dr. Pancake, "I love her dearly, consumingly, without sense (or nonsense, actually), and there is great definition in that sort of love, wouldn't you agree, Doctor?"

She gave him her pious grin, which made him feel queasy and subservient. "Piffle," she said, and dismissed him until the following week: as he walked out the door, she called, "Your last check bounced, Mr. Grimm. Please make it right."

epistobel and
the continuing
dissolution of
subatomic structures

She is composed of subatomic structures, and that's nothing new. It's not that she's fading away, not that she's decomposing: she's not—we all are. At equal rates. So she's not (fading away, decomposing). As the people who wear small hats are fond of saying, everything's relative. (If everything in the universe—galaxies, stars, nebulae, little puppies, atoms, clapboards, light bulbs, old men, potholders and widgets, *everything*—were expanding at the same rate, how would we know? And what would all of it be expanding into? And would anything be expanding at all?)

But why think about such things? It's sophomoric.

"That's sophomoric," said the comely young thing I've recently named Epistobel.

"No it isn't," I said. "It's profound."

She took my tray. I'd eaten everything—peas and ham slices and Jello (green, red, white), and pint of chocolate milk. I had been hungry; *(insertion of semicolon)* I was no longer hungry. My stomach felt full and I felt sated. Feeling sated is a good thing. It makes my necessary post-existence more doable. She gave me her falsely obsequious smile. I hate it. She said, "Go to sleep, Happy. It's the best time."

"Well now," I said to her back (as she left the room), "that's certainly cryptic. You can't simply say something cryptic and then make your exit. It's what cowards do." She was at the door: she turned only her head to look at me; she was still smiling, but it was not her falsely obsequious smile, it was an ugly smile that turned sharply up at the corners of her mouth and revealed a world of darkness within; it was the way a tree frog smiles. Then she made her exit.

Well, you know, that was a long time ago. I think it may have been hours ago; perhaps it was days ago. And she hasn't returned. I have to ask myself if she ever will. I need to be open to the grim possibility that she won't.

xiiv

She won't.

She can't.

She won't.

No mere grim possibility. A certainty, certainly.

Bob will come and go, and so, as well, the others who crowd past my doorway, pausing (some of them) to look in here and give me odd stares (questioning, critical, usually), but there will be no new Epistobel to bring me ham slices and grant me her cleavage.

Good-bye, Epistobel.

iivvii

When I was standing next to my father's bed (I was quite young, I believe), as he lay near sleep, I whispered, "Dad, are you awake?" and when he didn't respond at once, I said again, "Dad are you awake?" and his eyes opened a very little—enough to let only a bit of light in, I think—then he sneezed softly (it was unproductive;

barely audible), grinned a bit (as if in response to his soft sneeze) and died. It (his dying) was as swift as the sneeze itself, and I knew at once that it had happened—I could see it (Death) all about him, as if the dense, dark and moist air in the room had suddenly cleared and morning had begun.

chapter three

Andrew Grimm met the curvaceous and flirtatious Lily Hand when she was fourteen and he had just turned sixteen. He was very tall and thin, though passably attractive, in a loping, self-conscious way. He guessed generally, then, that he was very horny and that Lily was not. How could she be? She was a young female in a decade when females never even said the word "horny," a decade when they "performed their duty," and "did what was right for their husbands." Andrew thought he wanted Lily to do what was right for him, though, of course, he wasn't her husband, he was only an acquaintance with sweaty palms. He didn't, however, know for certain how she was going to "perform her duty" on him because he knew only as much about sex as he knew about advanced calculus, and he knew only as much about advanced calculus as it took to pull a consistent C-plus.

Lily's first words to him were, "Oh, that's a good, strange name," and offered Andrew her hand, which he took.

"'Andrew's a strange name?" he said.

"Grimm," she said. "That's a strange name. It's like the Grimm's fairy tales. I love them. They're not really like cartoon fairy tales at all."

He nodded, let go of her hand, realized *his* hand had been too moist, wondered if she'd noticed, looked briefly at his hand, thought she'd see he was looking at his hand, looked her in the eye ("Always look people in the eye," his mother told him. "That way, you'll know them, and they'll *know* you know them."), and said, "I read one once."

"Which one?" she said, and gave him an appealing smile—a bit of question, a bit of concern, a bit more than a bit of coquettishness.

"I don't know," he said. "I can't remember the title. It was very sad. I think it was about a little girl who sold matches."

"And died selling them, actually," Lily said. "But that wasn't The Brothers Grimm, it was Hans Christian Andersen. It was called, 'The Little Match Girl.' And yes, it was very sad. Terribly sad. So sad it made me cry."

He nodded, remembered that he, too, had cried a little when he'd read the story, remembered his father had noticed his tears, and said, "What's making you cry?" and remembered he'd answered, "This little story." When his father saw what the story was, he said it was all right, that he (the father) had cried upon reading it, too.

Now, years later, he (Andrew) said to Lily Hand, "It made me want to cry, too. But I didn't."

"I wouldn't expect that you would," she said, and gave him a smile, this time, that was mostly coquettish. It was an answer he liked, a smile he loved.

When he looked at her, he concentrated mostly on her eyes and her flushed cheeks: he glanced very quickly, though not often, at the rest of her, though only when she looked away momentarily. He imagined that her body was fully developed because—beneath her white, knit sweater and baggy jeans, cuffs rolled—it looked fully developed, and this urged him toward an erection. He covered it with a copy of *A Tale of Two Cities* he'd been reading for pleasure, but then he thought she'd noticed what he was doing, so he quickly uncovered his growing erection, glanced down at himself, saw little, and held his book at his side, which, he'd been told, was the only way boys *should* carry their books. (It was girls, after all, who carried their books in front.)

Lily said, "You want to go somewhere sometime? Like to a movie, maybe?"

Very quickly, he answered, "Yes, I do. Do you?" realized his mistake, and repeated, "Yes, I do," hesitated and added, "When? You mean like tonight, maybe?"

She sighed a little. "Well, some night. Maybe Friday," she said. "Tonight, I have to take care of my new kitten. She's sick, I think."

"You have a new kitten?" he said. "That's nice. A new kitten. I like kittens."

She nodded. "I named her Lilliputian. After me, more or less. 'Lily,' 'Lilliputian.' Get it? And after the story, too. *Gulliver's Travels*."

"Sure," he said. "*Gulliver's Travels*. I read it last year. I liked it a lot." He thought he was running off at the mouth. What if she asked him something about *Gulliver's Travels*? 'What did you like about it?' for instance. What would he say?

"No you didn't," she said, still smiling.

He felt himself blush.

"You're not a good liar, Andrew Grimm," she said. "Your eyes give you away."

"Yes," he said, and lowered his head a little, embarrassed. "I know. My mother says that all the time."

"And your father, too, I'm sure," said Lily Hand.

Andrew nodded glumly, but with a half-smile that he was sure would charm Lily. "And my father. He is, by the way, quite an accomplished liar."

"How do you know?" said Lily Hand.

Andrew thought about that and admitted that if someone "is truly an accomplished liar," then how could he (or anyone) know it? Oh, he liked Lily's mind as much, he was sure, as her consumable body.

note

I'm not Epistobel, though I exist. Happy Farmer exists, too. And the blue canoe, the vixen in estrous who's made her home in an upstairs room, the dog who would be Bob had he been Bob, the bats that flutter past the open door several times a day (a true horror show).

He forgets what's real, this man. I'm not sure why. Perhaps he prefers his fantasies. There's nothing wrong with that. We'd be nowhere without fantasies. We'd be jogging in place.

iixivii

This oblong room is my own and I exist alone in it. No one shares it with me, nor have I invited anyone to share it. I'm very jealous of my room: it feels, has always felt (through the long years) like an extension of the space my body uses, thus, when I find cryptic, vaguely challenging notes posted by others where only I have allowed myself to write, I feel I've been violated.

I see no one else here. A window, an open door. No one else but me.

iiivviiivv

Many hours later.

iiivviiivvi

I've been off in the blue canoe to the other side of the lake and up
the tall hill to the village or hamlet that exists there.

iiivviiivvii

All at once, my Roman numerals mystify me. They look like pillars. And I cannot, for the life of me, think of any number like
iiivviiivvii. Using the rules of Roman numerals, that would be
12, I believe. If you have a different idea, please let me know
ASAP. Contact me by letter, in care of the postmaster.

ix

A girl was there, in that village or hamlet. She stood behind an
ancient window that was distorted by age. I knocked softly on
the window when I first saw her (she was looking to her left,
away from me, toward a stand of pines), and I said, "Hello. Do
you live here?" But she simply looked at the pines.

She was a tall girl, and young. Thirteen, possibly. She was
wearing a long white dress. And, through the ancient, imperfect
window, she looked oblong, slanted, obscure. A painting of a girl.
A memory, perhaps, of a girl.

I said again, "Hello. Do you live here? I'm Happy Farmer. I
live across the lake."

She turned her head, then. Looked at me. Smiled slowly.

Then she mouthed three words. I couldn't hear them. I read
her lips. The words were, "I know you."

xiv

But who does? And who should? Who, among any of us, would want to be known by someone other than someone we love who also loves us? None of us. It's intrusive.

And that word encompasses a definition of this house and this room. It is an intrusive room. An intrusive house. Intrusive people exist in it.

I must leave. At once.

chapter four

He looked forward to her and to her body. He had decided that he saw her and her body as separate things. Her body knew nothing about judgment; her body knew only about lust, as did his: that was something, that was something! *She*, separate from her body, however, saw lust as necessary and vile, of course (it was what she'd been taught, what all of them had been taught, what she knew as fact, and he, too). So, over *here* (in the air, he supposed) *she* floated smilingly, angelically, and over here (on the ground, firmly) her body lay ready for his comfort and convenience. It wasn't headless, of course. It bore her head, her face on the head, her smile on the face—a lascivious, wondrous, carnal thing, her smile, a place of *becoming*.

She appeared at her door in answer to his knock. She was dressed for some awful food at a local restaurant called "PJ's Charbroil Ribs Pit," followed by a movie (*High Plains Drifter*) at The Capitol, in bright blue jeans (cuffs rolled), white tennis sneakers and a yellow, loose-fitting blouse (her blouses were always loose; they inexpertly hid her breasts).

"Andrew, why hello," she said. Bright, clear-eyed, smiling. He thought, *She's as beautiful as anything!*

He said, "Are you ready?" and hoped she caught his *double entendre*.

"I'm always ready," she said.

"Really?" he said.

She nodded enthusiastically. "I love the ribs at The Pit. Don't you?"

His shoulders dropped. He nodded a little. "Sure," he said, and sighed. "Sure," he repeated, and tried for an anticipatory smile. He hated the ribs at The Pit. He hated them so much, he thought he might become a vegetarian.

She came forward, slipped her slim arm in his, said cheerfully, "Well, then, let's go!"

He liked the feel of her arm—soft and warm. He thought of telling her so, started to speak, but she interrupted, "You smell good."

"I do?" he said.

She nodded. "Uh-huh."

"Gillette," he said. "It's the best aftershave," and rubbed his chin a little. He was glad she realized he was shaving, now.

She said nothing for a moment, then shook her head and said, "No, it's more like baby powder."

"Huh?" he said.

"Yeah," she said, and glanced up at him as they walked through the suburban night. "I know guys who use it."

He looked down at her. *As beautiful as anything!* he thought again. "You do?" he said.

A dog barked—once, and again. Fell silent. She said, "That's my neighbor's dog. He's nuts. He bites people for no reason."

"Why do they keep him?" Andrew asked.

She shrugged. "I don't know."

"Maybe they shouldn't keep him if he bites people."

"Maybe," she said.

He said, "What other guys do you know?"

She stopped walking. He stopped walking. Looked at her. "Something wrong?" he said.

"Why do you want to know about other guys in my life?" she said.

He could see her face poorly; he hadn't worn his glasses and it was evening and there were few streetlamps in the neighborhood—one every four or five houses. They were between streetlamps, now. He thought she was upset, that her lips were pursed. He said, "I was just wondering. I wasn't, you know, interested, like it was something I *needed* to know."

"Shit, too!" she said.

He'd never heard her swear before. He found it titillating. He hoped she'd swear again.

She said, "You're just wondering how many guys I've been out with. I can see it in your eyes." He'd heard this sort of thing before, from several people.

He said, "How can you see my eyes?"

"Huh?" she said.

"It's dark," he said. "So I don't think you can see my eyes, really. I can't see yours." It was true, though only because he wasn't wearing his glasses (they were brown, horn-rimmed; he didn't wear them because he thought they made him look like a fool).

"Well I can still see *your* eyes," she said. It's not *that* dark!"

"Oh."

"And I've been out with a few guys, if it's really your business." Brief pause. "And it isn't."

"How many?" he said, and realized his mistake at once. "Sorry," he added. "You don't have to answer that."

"Uh-huh," she said. "Well you *should* be sorry. And you're right—I don't have to answer it." A moment's silence. "Let's just go to The Pit and have some fucking food. I'm hungry!"

He smiled.

It was quite unfortunately true that he liked the women in his life to swear a lot, even his mother (though he knew that mothers were supposed to be above swearing and expressions of temper and various scatological *faux pas*: his mother was not above such things at all). It titillated him to hear women swear. He knew he was not alone in this—some of the guys he knew (in passing) at school enjoyed it, too. They were pretty brazen about why they liked it, as well, though Andrew preferred to keep his reasons to himself. He preferred keeping quite a lot to himself. For instance, what he did when he was alone.

One of the other guys—Stephen Baldo—asked him once, "What do you do when *you're* alone, Andrew?" Stephen was with a bunch of guys and they were all looking at Andrew with broad, anticipatory grins because he, Andrew, was the last in their all-male physics study group to have the question put to him.

Andrew shrugged, felt his face flush: he answered, "I don't know. Read, I guess. I read. And I play music."

"Fucking retard!" Howard Packer said. "Shit, Andrew, we told you what *we* do! Now it's your fucking turn!"

Andrew didn't like it when guys swore. He'd wondered *why* he didn't like it, but he had yet to come up with answers.

His father swore occasionally, though never "Fuck!"—only "Shit!" . . . "Damn!" . . . "Hell!" Tame stuff, Andrew thought. Why was his father so tame? he wondered. He'd be on his death-bed and someone would ask, "Why did you live such a tame life?" and he (Andrew's Father) would have no cogent answer, and the other person would add, "Well, it's a fucking shame."

Andrew didn't want to live a tame life but he thought he had no choice. He felt like a tame person. Other guys went to stores and shoplifted; he demurred. Other guys walked up to girls and said something really forward and suggestive ("Want to sit on my lap and talk about the first thing that pops up?" for instance, or "You must be tired—you've been running around in my mind all day.") but the most forward and suggestive words Andrew had ever uttered to a female he didn't yet know was, "Hi. My name's Andrew. People have told me I'm pretty wild." (To which the nameless female answered, "Are you sure?" and walked away.)

But there was that intrusive question—"What do you do when you're alone, Andrew?" and he didn't want to answer it because what he did when he was alone was, by definition, private, which was what he conjured up, now, to say to the all-male physics study group:

"Well, what I do when I'm alone is, by definition, private," which, of course, elicited loud guffaws and howling laughter which, because they were in the school library, got all seven of them booted out. Andrew had wanted to say, "I think about things like life and death and stuff," but he didn't because he wasn't sure it was true.

⚎

But it was true: he thought about death a lot when he was alone.

⚎

Dr. Amelia Pancake once told him his preoccupation with death was unhealthy. "What do you derive from this preoccupation?" she asked, and he told her gently that it wasn't really a preoccupation, it was simply an interest because, after all, death was something he ("Everyone, you know!") would face at some point, so he thought he needed to have some feelings and ideas stored away before Death, he explained, "pulls up to the curb and offers me a ride."

Dr. Pancake found the comment interesting, almost charming, but she didn't tell him so because she thought it might merely be a cheap salve to his ego, and cheap salves to the ego, in her opinion, amounted to no more than the temporary satisfaction of a bowl of ice cream. She gave him her best noncommittal smile, instead, and asked, "And what sorts of feelings and ideas have you stored away, Andrew?"

He told her he needed to end the session because he'd forgotten a dental appointment.

She gave him her all-knowing therapist smile and said, "You're an awful liar, Andrew."

"No," he said, "I'm an accomplished liar."

xivi

They have changed the name of the only restaurant in *the-town-named-after-the-lake*. It used to be "Donna's Eats 'n Hots," but now it's called "The Eatin' Hole," which I find grotesquely charming, but here's the thing: *(insertion of otherwise parenthetical statement)* when I went in for breakfast, there, yesterday morning, I recognized nothing—not the seats, not the floor or the ceiling or the lamps and homey framed prints of fantastical villages hidden in coves and forests, not the colors of the place, the people who worked there, the smells: it was also larger than I remember, which I could see from the outside: it was perhaps half again as large.

I asked one of the waitresses about it (she was a svelte, beer-colored woman whose name tag read "Dora"): "Have you rebuilt the place?" I said, and she gave me a crooked smile and an odd stare and said, "Not that I know of, Mister, and I've been here since Eisenhower."

I chuckled.

She didn't.

I ordered my usual breakfast—scrambled eggs, marmalade on wheat toast, regular coffee, grapefruit and a bowl of Wheaties—ate it hungrily and left the place.

Then I walked three miles to the blue canoe.

I went in it across the lake to the tall hill and, from there, made my way to the small village or hamlet, which was not empty, though it may as well have been.

There are Times in Our Lives (some of us, not all of us) when Our memories (the things we remember) become unreliable, when they assume multiple, disparate forms, and when they do (and they do because, I think, we age beyond the years (beyond the time) that nature, at our birth, granted us [some of us, not all of us]) these memories stop becoming enjoyable, or worthy, and become (at last) confusing, frustrating, even nightmarish, and so there we are, caught (through happenstance) beyond the age when death should have claimed us, in a hellish stew of memories we may or may not be parent to, and so we search everywhere for a good and proper place to die in order to escape those hellish memories. What else can we do? What choice do we have? But death has already forsaken us once. Odds are it will forsake us again.

iiiix

Droste, Holland—Pastilles milk
Pottery Barn—Made in China

Caution:
Use cr3202 battery.
Insert battery properly, observing polarity.

<u>*adjustable desk lamp*</u>
lampe reglable de pupitre

⛏

It is so good to celebrate, now and again, from time to time, when it presents itself earnestly, when there is no choice, the undeniably real.

The young girl behind the window was not the young girl I remembered: she was large-mouthed and small-eyed and she was dressed as if for a day of nothing more than writing in her diary. She cocked her head at me when I appeared on the day side of her window: "Who are you?" she hollered, and her voice was peaky and unnerving through the window glass.

I shook my head. I saw no reason to answer her.

Then someone I assumed was her mother appeared on the porch, from within the house. She was tall, thin, square-faced: she wore a long blue dress, and yellow apron, and her long, thin hands were covered with what I supposed was flour.

She said, "Do you want something here?"

I shook my head again.

"Why are you looking in that window?" she said.

"I wasn't actually looking *in* the window," I said.

I glanced at the window. The little girl had her nose pressed hard against it and her tongue stuck out so it was flat against the glass.

The woman I assumed to be the girl's mother said, "Then I'll ask again: what are you doing?"

"I'm doing nothing," I said.

"That's a silly and stupid answer," the woman said. She gave me a stern look. "It is impossible to do nothing, especially when it involves others, especially when you have clearly come a long, long way."

I gestured toward the lake, which wasn't visible through the pines. "I come only from the hill across the lake."

Her brow furrowed. She said, "You're wrong. There is no lake."

"But there is," I said.

She glared at me.

"I've been canoeing on it many times," I said.

"Be that as it may," she said, "it's gone now. And for decades, too." She looked at the window that the girl I assumed to be her daughter stood behind and yelled, "Get away from there! You don't know what in the hell you'll see!" turned quickly and went back into her house.

ixiivxi

I mean, Son, my father wrote, *Death is no great emancipator, no great transformer; it does not charm us, caress us or give us succor from the tribulations of the living: Death simply is. And what do we know of it, its properties, its parameters, its needs and desires? It's foolish even to ask such questions. And their answers, if there are any, are of no real concern to me: You see, death is nothing.*

My father wrote that way a lot. Always so earnest and anachronistic in his writing style: he taught me nothing that I want to emulate.

But I think, now, here, in this huge house, of Epistobel and her quiet grave behind the silent village and I want more for her, and (so) more for myself; it's my due, after all. All of us are due more by this universe and its alleged creator than a quiet grave that rests behind a silent village.

The comely young thing who brings me my food and occasionally tells me secrets has made no appearance in days.

If I were the type to feel lonely I would feel *very* lonely.

Bob zips past my door, then back again—too fast to be of much importance.

chapter five

He thought he knew next-to-nothing about sex, but he was wrong. He knew very little, but it wasn't "next-to-nothing": it was, in fact, more than others his age knew—male or female—though he hadn't taken a poll, hadn't asked anyone in his small group of friends (who were mostly, he'd have been the first to happily admit, not "friends," per se, but acquaintances) what they knew, what their thoughts were, how they approached the whole fascinating, maddening, mysterious, forbidden subject (sex) and, at last, how they (some of them) had dealt with actually *having* it. He thought that none of them *actually* had: he harbored the unspoken belief that nearly everyone (perhaps, indeed, *everyone*) in his group had yet to lose his or her virginity and that their swaggers, twitters, and braggadocio were simply a lot of damned bullshit.

So when it came time for him to, as he wrote, "relieve myself of my burdensome virginity," he was happy it wasn't with the angelic Lily Hand, whom he was certain he loved (and how could his first bumbling, barely post-pubescent sexual encounter be with someone he actually loved? Good Lord, she'd lock herself in the bathroom and beg never to see him again.); it was with a young woman named Jessica Mandolar, who was tall, a little plump, very, very blond, and who spoke mostly in words of one syllable.

He found himself pitying her, and hating it (the fact that he pitied her): he pitied her because she was, as far as he could see at his age (and as he wrote), "locked in a box of ignorance, stupidity and lascivious needs," which (the lascivious needs) he was only too-happy to service, notwithstanding her obvious ignorance and stupidity.

And service her needs he did—with great, barely post-pubescent, fumbling urgency, as if his life could go no further should he choose to keep his pants zipped.

Out of courtesy, at least, he thought he should take some time with her blouse buttons, which were complex hook-and-eye affairs, not real buttons, but he glanced at her face as he unsuccessfully twisted her complex hooks this way and that, saw that she was becoming impatient (the set of her jaw said it all, he told himself later) and decided to simply rip the damned blouse from her body, and so he did, much, he believed at the time, to her "happy dismay" (as he wrote later), and then found himself confronted by her mammoth dark blue bra and its equally complex array of straps and fasteners, so he merely lifted the thing up, toward her gentle neck (she was beneath him, on her large bed, in her huge house, while her parents watched "I Love Lucy" two floors below), which (as he wrote later) "released her incredibly satisfying, appealing, and arousing glands" and, upon catching sight of her nipples (the first he had seen which were not his mother's or his sister's), shot his wad in one long, death-defying shriek that stopped the parental laughter on the first floor and brought both parents at a galumphing run up the stairs as if the house were on fire.

"Oh, good Lord, shit, damn!" said Jessica Mandolar monosyllabically, as her parents burst into the room, saw their daughter and Andrew Grimm straight-arming one another on her bed (though neither parent knew that Andrew had merely let go in his pants), and wept.

xix

I believe this house is changing. I believe that it is either growing or shrinking and, until I leave this room, it will be impossible for me to know which it is doing:

I can't say why I believe this. I dreamt about it, which could have something to do with my new conviction. I dreamt that it was shrinking and growing at the same time, and that would be impossible, of course, because nothing shrinks and grows at the same time (but this may not be true. In various ways, people themselves shrink and grow at the same time all their lives, from birth to death: but that could merely be intellectual and philosophical sophistry, which I eschew).

It came to me that it was shrinking because, at one point, Bob the dog *(formerly "the-dog-who-would-have-been-Bob-had-he-been-Bob")* zipped past my open door, but not so quickly that I couldn't see he was smaller than I remembered. Since he could not have been physically smaller than the last time I'd seen him (perhaps weeks earlier), I guessed that the *doorway* had grown larger. And if the doorway had grown larger, it would have to mean that the *house itself* had grown larger.

Minutes later, however, Bob again zipped past my doorway, in the opposite direction, and it was clear, then, that *he* was larger than when I'd last seen him (weeks earlier). And I realized that if he were actually larger then it would mean that the doorway had grown *smaller*, which meant the *house* had grown smaller.

And my question, now (hours later) is this: if the house is indeed either shrinking or growing (or both), then *what* is happening to *me?*

Oh, this existence I've inherited (due to unforeseen circumstances) is chock full of good, unanswerable questions.

ix

Some things are important, other things aren't. It's something my father used to tell me. "Some things, Happy, are important. Other things aren't." And every time he said it, I said, "Yes, I know. It's obvious," and he said, with one of his Daddy smiles, "Well, son, some things are obvious, I suppose, but not most things, perhaps very few things. Perhaps, Happy, *nothing* is obvious, and if we spend our lives believing otherwise then we're wasting the precious time that life itself has granted us."

Believe me, because it's true, he repeated that speech verbatim countless times, not just to me but to my brothers and sisters, my mother, people he worked with (they told me about the speech; some called it "erudite," some "profound," others did not) and *his* father and mother, *his* brothers and sisters, et cetera, et cetera. And so I have recalled it here word for word.

epistobel
and the grave

Nothing exists more obvious than a grave. Not a smile, nor a sneer, nor bad news. A grave lies obvious. It whispers loud. It focuses the attention as nothing else. *I am here. I am here. I am nowhere.*

Epistobel talked about death but did not like to; she said, "Death is a bad topic."

She died one day without expecting it. No one did. She woke in the morning and lived through midday, till 3:36—a fine afternoon, except for her death.

She said to me, before she died, "I want you to know that I am not very happy." It was the last thing I heard from her, and she said it in response to some misdeed I can't remember, though I remember her final words (which are, after all, more important).

When someone dies whom you love or feel you will love or, you're certain, will grow to control your life—whether you love them to the point of incoherence and obsession or not—I think you never find your way again.

Perhaps that's why I'm here, in this house that's growing and shrinking at the same time.

Zip Bob by the open door. Zip Bob back! Small dog, big dog, same dog.

Same dog?
For Christ's sake, whose universe *is* this?

epistobel
and the slippery
dance of time

Epistobel and Irene the murder victim, killed by Dave in a pique of jealousy and (according to local gossip) soul-destroying frustration, knew one another as children and then again when they were both in their 20s and nearing their denouement.

I knew Irene only in the last year or so of her existence, when she lived across the street from us in a modest green frame house, with four cats and a miniature white poodle named Spring, who bit strangers and pissed on the rugs.

Irene spoke to me just rarely, and when she did it was usually a complaint: "Do you know that your mother gardens in her bra, Happy?" she said once, and I could only nod and grin foolishly. And, "Do you know that your mother brays like a mule at night, Happy?" to which I could, also, only nod and grin foolishly.

I saw Epistobel go into Irene's house on a day that threatened rain and snow, and I saw her leave Irene's house an hour later with a bouquet of red flowers and Spring the miniature poodle on a leash.

I didn't know Epistobel, then, as well as I would one day.

It occurs to me, now, that I didn't know her at all.

xxi

It *occurs* to me, goddammit, that none of what I've written under the heading above ("Epistobel and The Fucking Slippery Dance of Time") is true, or real.

It occurs to me that I'm coming apart.

If I go to the open door and look left and right, what will I see?

Perhaps I'm unwilling to find out.

Perhaps there's much more to the end of existence than I had ever considered possible.

ixii

Hallway. Hallway. Both empty. Empty.

Houses in the midst of change. All houses. A universe of houses. What in this inestimable universe is without continuous change in the slippery dance of time?

He put it that way and I thought it was lyrical, almost erudite, almost profound: "We are doing a slippery dance in time," he said, and gave me one of his many smiles.

"In time with what?" I said, feeling clever.

"In time with *time*," he said, as if my question had been stupid. I can hear him now, so many odd years later, so much muck under the bridge: "In time with *time*, and time *leads*," he said. Grizzled old fruitcake, playing with my philosophies.

Epistobel invited me to have her whenever I wanted her, whenever I needed her, which are one and the same, and I took her many, many times, and in many, many places—in libraries and pool halls and in parking garages and the closets of friends, *in* beds and *beside* beds and on top of various kinds of dresser drawers (with mirrors and without, as well), in trailers and on top of schools and in orchards of all kinds, and also in vineyards, which are sweet smelling.

She smelled sweet all over, too, from her forehead to her belly and her insistent vagina and her brown nipples and her round white thighs and her toes, her soles, her acceptable knees.

She was to womanhood the whole of womanhood and she knew it, though she never said it, and I never said it to her: *(insertion of colon)*

In the midst of lovemaking, she might say, "I love what this body allows me." It was something she said a half dozen times during our long relationship, and always when I was inside her and she was riding me. And this, too: "I wish there really were some creature who was the creator of all this and I would thank it unceasingly."

She was terse always in her speech, but never in her lovemaking, which tossed sleep aside and brought all kinds of exquisite pain.

We never rested, she and I.

I think often of her bones and her decaying parts.

I'll have to read from the beginning, now, and find out where they're buried: I've noted it, I know—somewhere in these few pages.

chapter six

Not long into their separation he hired a detective to find her and tell her how much he missed her. The detective's name was Fred Spoon and he was as tall as a doorway and lived in a six story house. He smoked 100mm cigarettes and spoke in unending sentences. One of those sentences, in paraphrase here, told Andrew that Lily Hand was nowhere to be found, that she had apparently slipped off into some alternate dimension, which Andrew found not very funny or helpful, and he told Fred Spoon he wasn't going to pay him, so Fred Spoon beat the shit out of Andrew and left him in an alley, between a dark green dumpster and a sleeping Chinese man who was down on his luck.

When the Chinese man woke up, he found that Andrew needed attention and summoned the police, who summoned an ambulance, who took Andrew straightaway to St. Stanislaus' Hospital, on Heatherberry Street, where Andrew was put into intensive care. It was where he met Dr. Grace Althaway, who gave him the very best of care and then invited him to her house for sushi, custard pie, and a night of "preternaturally satisfying sex." Andrew thanked her effusively, but demurred: "My heart lies with another," he said, and Dr. Althaway gave him a look he couldn't decipher, and sighed. She called him a shithead, but she had her back turned, so he didn't hear her.

He telephoned Fred Spoon and made his apologies. Spoon apologized too. "I don't usually beat people up just because they don't pay me," he said. "But I've had a bad year. My rent's due, all my magazine subscriptions are running out, my tires are down to the nub, and I haven't had a good cheeseburger in a month and a half." Andrew said he understood, added that he'd been given very adequate care at St. Stanislaus Hospital, then begged Spoon to look, again, into the whereabouts of the missing Lily Hand.

Spoon said, "You going to pay me first?"

Andrew said, "I'll send you a check. Deposit it on Friday, okay?"

"Sure," Spoon said.

A week later, he showed up at Andrew's door with a mile-wide grin (a 100mm cigarette stuck out one side of it), and said, "You're something, Mr. Grimm. You are really something. I beat the living vahoosma out of you and you hire me again."

"Did my check clear?" Andrew asked.

Spoon nodded. "Uh-huh," he said, and nodded to indicate the inside of the house. "Do you mind? It's cold."

Andrew let him in and they sat in Andrew's living room, which was decorated tastefully in rich reds and greens and which had multiple photographs and paintings of the exquisite Lily Hand all about.

Andrew said, " 'Vahoosma'?"

Spoon said, smiling, "It's the word my sainted mother used instead of 'shit.'"

Andrew said, "I like it. It's cool. I like it a lot."

one

On a foggy morning late in October, many years ago, and through
no one else's urging, I came to this cavernous house in a mammoth Chevy Caprice.

I have worked tirelessly ever since.

I've added up the events and detritus of the lives I may have
lived and have attempted to make sense of them.

I've made sense of nothing.

I've prayed for understanding of all that I don't understand
(which is most things, perhaps all things), though I admit that I
never understood or accepted the necessity of prayer.

I accept the existence of all things.

I accept that reality is a stew made of rumors and rust.

I accept that love comes from within and without and that we
owe it our lives and our good sense.

I know that Epistobel exists as surely as any fact I have lain
down in the pages of this narrative.

I admit that her kisses, her embraces and her sweet vagina
have hobbled me and made me worthless.

I believe that I may exist, now, in a realm which defies all
understanding and which is the source of a world full of dogma,
confusion, and fantasy.

Back from The Eatin' Hole. Had lunch there. What a good lunch—salad greens and mixed fruits, plus a tuna rollup which was to-die-for.

As well, the waitress, who introduced herself as Linnea, was as friendly as a used car salesman and as appealing as a new apple, which was just the kind of friendliness I needed today, the day after Bob's death.

I did not see him die. I intuited his death. I saw him run past my doorway—in the quick, purposeful but mindless way he has always run past my doorway—and then, when he didn't run back, I understood and accepted that he had died and had been buried not far from this house, under a small plot of winter grass, *sans* headstone or marker.

Two stories below my window, now, a chorus of shrill voices rises like an awful heat and gives me a painful embrace.

I recognize all the voices, can focus on no single voice.

This place is a crazy quilt of contradictions which are, of course, contradictions only in another universe, where there has been, for millennia, a very different way of making sense, a universe that operates not nearly as free of rules and of order as this universe does.

Take my watch.

The clock chimes.

I grab my cock and spin. *(Insertion of chapter break.)*

chapter seven

(The writer looks backward and attempts to make sense of the ridiculous, which, by his definition, encompasses all he has not understood, or, if he has understood, the things which made his life full of peaks and valleys, exhaustion and sexual exaspera-tion. He has so very much simply wanted to sleep well, at least once.

And so, now, the things which may have been true.)

Fred Spoon, private dick, was a man of questionable taste. His cigarettes smelled like old shoes and his six-story house looked like it had been built of lumber, clapboards and drywall he'd rummaged from a house in ruin.

He invited Andrew Grimm to sit on a Mediterranean-style sofa that looked as uncomfortable as a shoeless man, and Andrew said, "No, thank you. I'll stand," though he was tired and very much needed to sit.

Fred Spoon shrugged, nodded at a tall stool across the large room, and invited Andrew to sit on it, which Andrew did: Spoon sat on the couch and lit a cigarette, which he kept at one side of his mouth as he talked, so it bobbed in time with his words.

He said, "Names are so unimportant, really, when one has stopped existing, don't you think?" He paused, as if for a response from Andrew, but then went on, "But her name, at any rate, was Irene and she owned a house not far from here."

Andrew nodded. He'd heard of Irene.

"And her lover did her in not long ago," Spoon said, and leaned forward so his elbows were on his knees. He raised a hand and touched his long cigarette, but he didn't take it from his mouth. He lowered his hand. "Her lover slashed her throat with a large kitchen knife," he added, and smiled a little.

"Jeez," said Andrew.

Spoon nodded, "Yes, awful," he said. "And, at any rate, you know, I've been asked to look into the matter. For insurance purposes."

"Oh?" said Andrew, who found the tall stool as uncomfortable as a woman without knees.

Spoon nodded earnestly. "Insurance purposes, yes," he said. "It's always about money, I think. Don't you? Always about the getting of the green and the acquisition of power and the satiation of greed."

Andrew found himself awfully impressed by Spoon's verbal abilities. He hadn't expected it. Spoon had seemed like such a dullard.

Spoon went on, "And this slashing of Irene's throat: my God, Andrew, you should have been there! It was a thing as awful as the caterwauling of bears and ocelots. Blood splattered everywhere, on pots and pans and dishes and butter servers, you know. What a mess! And that's not even to mention her suffering—*Irene's* suffering. You probably think it leads to a damned quick death, the slashing of a throat. You go to a movie and you see it on the screen and you see the victim, there, grab her throat and fall, *Kerplunk!*, dead to the floor. But it doesn't happen that way in what passes for the real world, Andrew. Not, at any rate, in *this* world."

two

She turned her head. Looked at me. Smiled slowly.

Then she mouthed three words. I couldn't hear them. I read her lips. The words were, "I know you."

But I didn't know her, and if I *did* know her, I wasn't aware of it.

She mouthed these words, "I'm part of you. *We're* part of you."

"*We're* part of you" was how she said it. She and the others whom I have yet to meet, in that little village or hamlet, that small place, that universe, are all a part of me. *Were* a part of me.

The late afternoon sun reflected sharply from the window she stood behind and I lost her for a moment: I stepped to my left, found her again, behind the window, watching me, head upturned slightly because I was taller: she put her hand flat on the window, glanced at it, looked at me again. I thought there was some significance in what she was doing, some significance in her hand on the window.

She mouthed these words: "You look only backward, Happy."

It astounded me that she knew my name.

She took her hand from the window, raised the other, put it flat against the window, looked at it.

The sun on the window stole her from me again. I moved left, found her once more—her hand on the window, her head turned upward to me. She mouthed these words: "What do you *have?*"

I thought fleetingly, *At this moment, I have only the sunlight, the still, warm air, the near and distant sounds of insects and birds, you*—meaning her, the one behind the window.

She smiled as if I had spoken to her. Dropped her hand. Moved back from the window, into the bowels of the little house.

Significant freezing rain falls as I type. It laces the evergreens and the bare branches of the oaks and tulip trees near the house, and the porch roof has become coated with it. It's already thick enough that I can hear it crackling under its own weight. It's nearly as translucently beautiful as an exquisitely beautiful woman.

I taught English at a junior college once, a five-year stint I despised because I didn't know how to teach kids who were a mixture of those who really wanted to learn and those who were getting a degree simply because having to work at a fast food joint made them depressed.

Such goddamned lucid writing, as if I'm actually talking about my past. And my present.

Junior college? Which one? So many. Probably hundreds.

Who cares?

It might be true.

As true as this: Bob and Epistobel are dead.

I await the return of the comely young thing, who brings my meals on a happy schedule.

ixiiivi

I believe this: We become schedules. We become outlines, plans, dogma, memos, facts. And all of that stuff becomes pillars for our biological selves so we can pretend to spirituality or, at least, pretend to some existence beyond the corporeal. But what we don't know, what our memos, facts and outlines don't tell us, is this: we don't have even the corporeal.

At least some of us, unnamed, don't.

Perhaps only the unnamed (who are, of course, the anonymous, who are, of course, those who do not exist, which seems, on the very face of the phrase itself, like an oxymoron, but it isn't; it merely speaks of what has past which will never pass again).

iiii

It seems reasonable.

It's what Father used to say. In his way. Now he floats cosmically nowhere, and I'm sick of it.

> *Yesterday, upon the stair,*
> *I met a man who wasn't there.*
> *He wasn't there again today.*
> *Oh, how I wish he'd go away.*

⚷

Ah, there she is, the comely young thing I once named Epistobel, who is now—and of her own choice—anonymous, with my evening meal.

I smile: I am a happy animal.

chapter four

Detective Fred Spoon owned a gun but he kept it locked in a storage cabinet in his basement because he was afraid of it. "It fired all by itself once," he said. "I wasn't anywhere near it. It was on my coffee table: I thought it looked neat next to my magazines— you know, *American Spectator* and *The Wall Street Journal*, that kind of stuff—and I had a lady friend with me whose name was Gladys, real stacked, like any woman named Gladys has to be, you know, and she was pointing at the gun and I was smiling this real shit-eating kind of grin because I knew *she* knew the lore about guns and penises, and she rubs up against me, you know, with her bosoms and her pubic area at the same time, so it got me, you know, real hot, and when I got real hot, and I started to sweat, the damned gun went off and shot Gladys in the foot, for Christ's sake, in her right heel, and shattered it, so she hasn't been right with that heel ever since, poor thing."

Spoon told me all of this as I sat on his very uncomfortable Mediterranean-style sofa and held a glass of ginger ale which had doubtless gone flat days earlier. He sat on a tall stool not far off, feet on the stool's first rung, back hunched over: he also had a glass of ginger ale in hand which, thankfully, was empty, because he gesticulated wildly as he talked.

He said, "You like the ginger ale? Sorry it's flat. I like it flat, but I think I'm the only one in the world who does. Fizzy bubbles make me nervous, you know. Are you like that?"

I started to say, *No, I'm not,* but he hurried on, "And well, this woman named Gladys and me, we don't see each other much anymore, only when she's missing my prowess in bed, you know."

I nodded.

He said, "I'll tell you about it sometime, okay? Great story. Lots of stories, really. I'll tell you them sometime." He paused very briefly. "Now what did you say the name of the woman was who you're looking for? Agnes?"

"Agnes?" I said.

He shook his head vigorously, frowned. "No, don't tell me. I know it's not Agnes. I forget things, you know. What was it? What was it? Her name. Tell me."

"Lily Hand," I said.

He cocked his head. "Odd name. Hand. I don't think I've heard of anyone by that name. You sure that's her name?"

"I'm sure," I said.

"Good. Then we'll mount a search at once."

xi

I asked the comely young thing whom I'd named Epistobel, but who was, again, and simply, *the comely young thing*, "Who are those people down there?"—meaning the people below my window who were invisible to me behind the front porch roof.

The comely young thing said she didn't know who they were but if they were bothering me, she'd ask them to go away.

"I can hardly sleep with all that noise!" I said.

"I understand," she said. "But do you really think you *need* to sleep anymore, Happy?"

I hadn't the foggiest idea what she meant. Of course I needed to sleep, if only to dream: in the course of my four or five decades on the earth, I have learned that, for a lot of people, dreams are the *only* reason for sleep.

The comely young thing added wistfully, "Or *dream*, for that matter, Happy. Or *eat*?" She gave me a smile I could not interpret.

"We all need to eat," I said.

"I don't," she said. "So why should you?"

How, I wondered, could I answer her question? It was foolish.

"Happy, the question isn't at all foolish," she said. "But it *is* rhetorical." She flashed another wistful smile.

"My God," I said, "you're reading my mind!"

"Not at all," she said. "I'm reading *you*."

☿—

The clock chimes.

☿—

I need music. I have none. I need Vivaldi. Queen. Grieg. The Rolling Stones. I need pancakes. And music.

☿—

Death, my father wrote, *Happy, is not at all like moving from the bright and living air into an oblong box. It's very different from that. We are victims (all of us, even the brightest of us) of our petty intellects and outlooks and fears. It makes our existence less endurable and we concoct comforting fantasies so we can look forward to much, much more than we honestly (and, indeed, intellectually) expect from the end of existence. But, as it turns out, Death is a way around the real oblong box.*

My father wrote well, and honestly, but I think he knew little, or nothing, about anything at all. He'd agree with that, of course. Quickly and easily.

☿—

In order there is predictability, he wrote. *In predictability there is security.*

172 | *t.m. wright*

I need music and pancakes. I need arithmetic. I need trademarks and rough wood. I need a sunset, a sunrise, a beautiful woman, a caress or two. A carafe of something potable. Something red will do.

I have never seen a face in a casket. I have avoided funerals throughout my life. I've been invited to them, been told about them and told, also, how nice it would be to attend, to show my respects, to bid farewell. But it seems useless, even self-serving, to bid fucking *farewell* to anyone. Where does anyone go that they cannot, in some way, return? We hear music once, then again, and again, over the space of months or years—the same music, the same tune, for instance "Rockabye Sweet Baby James," or, perhaps, "Appalachian Spring," or "Revolution"—and do we bid it farewell, even when we're very old and can hear nothing but our own eardrums making a constant high-pitched noise? Of course not.

I know this, so believe me: *Pepsi is the real thing* and *Nothing succeeds like success.*

I have somewhere to go, I know, and so it is time for that. Eventually.

chapter six

Fred Spoon thought the first place to look for Lily Hand was in the green, two-story Cape Cod she owned on Maple, so we went there on a Thursday that threatened rain and broke in through an open first-floor window. She wasn't in the house, though we searched tirelessly ("I've knocked on her door many times, Mr. Spoon," I said), so we went to her place of employment, "John's Rentals," on Elm, and Spoon interrogated John himself for many minutes until he told us, reluctantly, that she had quit her position (Senior File Enabler) several weeks earlier to become a lounge singer in Connecticut.

"Oh yeah," Spoon growled. "Where in Connecticut?"

"Winooski," John managed.

"That's in Vermont!" Spoon reminded him tersely.

"Is it really?" John said, clearly surprised. "She told me it was in Connecticut."

Spoon turned to me and said, "Things are looking very weird, Andrew."

iixxii

I had known Lily Hand for ten months; we'd met at a breakfast joint named "Eggs and So Forth," on Oak: she was between jobs and I was at Eggs and So Forth putting up flyers advertising a new burlesque called "Nearly Next to Nude." She approached me as I was taping one of the flyers on the inside of a front window and said, "Are they nude there, in that place?"

I glanced quizzically at her and said, "Nude?"

She smiled, clearly amused. "Yes. Naked. Without clothes. If they are, the city fathers will be upset."

I shook my head vigorously. "No, not at all. They're, uh"—I nodded at the flyer—"*Nearly Next to Nude*, which"—I smiled—"sort of says it all, don't you think?"

She shrugged. "Not really. What the hell does that mean—'Nearly Next to Nude'—anyway?"

I shrugged too, and, moments later, we were each enjoying a stack of pancakes with real maple syrup and talking with great animation about love and death and good cooking.

xxiii

"Have you noticed," said Fred Spoon, "that whatever the hell we do, it always uses up time."

"Is that a question?" I said.

"It's something like a question," he said. He'd fallen and scraped his knee badly: he was covering the knee with a healing lotion, which he would follow with a wide bandage.

We were in Vermont, had been nearing Winooski, when his accident happened.

epistobel insinuates herself upon reality

This room is long and narrow and without windows on its south and north sides. A chiming clock sits on one wall and several paintings on the other. All of these paintings are my own; I've reproduced several of them in this narrative.

Epistobel sat nude for me once. She did it happily, even lustily, which made *me* happy and lustful as well.

I don't own the painting which resulted from that sitting, though I remember it, and, therefore, could reproduce it here if I wanted— if I felt it would be an invaluable part of this narrative, if I thought Epistobel herself would not find its display embarrassing.

Even the dead find embarrassment in the overt and purposeless violation of their privacy and dignity. I've learned this. My father spoke of it often.

Irene, for instance. When he saw her being carried off on a gurney, under a dark green morgue blanket, he said, "They should put her hand on her stomach. It's only right. Give her some damned privacy." He was sentimental like that sometimes.

He was the same way when my mother died. He saw her lying on the road, not far from the car that had run her down, and he blubbered, "Oh God, why do they leave her uncovered, Happy? Why do they let her lie there exposed?" I had no answer.

If I left this room, where would I go? Would I find adventure? Would I find people I don't know, and lands I've yet to explore, beyond that doorway?

I live on foolishness, I think.

This room has never been my prison.

Hear this: the blue canoe exists. It was manufactured by Tuft Industries, in Gary, Indiana. It's twelve feet long, two and a half feet wide at its widest point, and its original color was red, which you can see in quarter-inch wide strips just under the gunwales. Sid took good care of the canoe, stored it in a shed in the winter and, in the summer, kept it on cinder blocks, under a tarp, so the sun wouldn't bleach the paint or buckle the wood (which is birch).

I found the room where the fox makes its den. It's on the third floor, as rumor (from the others) suggests, halfway down an unlighted corridor that runs north/south; the room has no door, which allows the fox to come and go as it pleases. I didn't see the fox there, though I smelled it—a strong, musky odor I first smelled when I was a child and I nearly tripped over a vixen and its cubs in a thicket not far from our farmhouse.

Our lives consist primarily of repetition. Our deaths, too. Repetition soothes us; we find order in it.

epistobel and the dissolution of sub-atomic structures

She sat nude with great discomfort. She was shy, found embarrassment in mundane things—her large hands, her sacral dimples, walking in sunlight without a hat, being without Kleenex, sighing, sweating, becoming horny.

"This is making me horny, Happy," she said when she was sitting for me, and her entire body blushed. She was seated in a way that exposed little—the side of her breast, the curve of her ass. It was a pose which I'd suggested: "There's so much more in a whisper than in a shout!" I pontificated.

"Not always," she said. "Not for everyone."

"Not for everyone, true. But it is for me," I said.

"No, I don't think so," she said

I found her comments annoying.

She lies cold and inaccessible in a small cemetery a thousand feet south of Centerville, New York. She shares the cemetery with 17 others, though the names of only three of those others are readable—a woman named Bonnie, who, according to her headstone, was "Wife of Charles Quint" (apparently buried somewhere else), Sergeant William Bodene, of the Second Calvary, who died of cholera sometime in the 1860's (the date is all but unreadable), and "F. Cucchiaio," born, says his or her headstone, in Italy in

1872. That's it. Four lousy graves. Epistobel's is marked only by a flat gray stone with the letters "I. G." etched deeply into it.

"Do you want to make love?" I said to her.

"No, you're painting," she said.

"I can stop painting," I said.

"I enjoy being horny; it's all right," she said. "Paint me. Just paint me. Then I'll leave."

"We're not going to make love? I thought you were horny."

"We'll make love another time," she said. "Tomorrow, perhaps. I'll come back tomorrow and sit for you again, then we'll make love."

"Why not today *and* tomorrow?" I said.

"Just paint," she said.

I've been to her grave fourteen times. I haven't returned to it in many years. It's true, of course, that she lies alone there—except for Bonnie Quint , Sergeant Bodene, F. Cucchiaio and fourteen others unnamed and unnamable who share the same two-thirds of an acre, but who can say that any of these people are good company? She's intelligent and has good taste. She plays piano as if her fingers were designed for nothing else. She smiles in a way that says she isn't alone at all.

Listen to her name: *Epistobel.* You've known no one by that name, so don't even wrack your brain trying to remember. It was her mother's invention: she felt it meant "flowing beauty," although, according to Epistobel herself, she had no reason for believing this, only that the name sounded as if it *should* mean "flowing beauty."

"You're a beauty," I told her while she was sitting for me.

"A folded beauty," she said with a smile, because of the position I'd put her in.

Perhaps she *was* Epistobel, after all.

I'm in a room that's no more than a box and I'm mortally confused.

chapter seven

What concerned Fred Spoon most about the disappearance of Lily Hand was its juxtaposition (in time) to a series of grisly murders which took place in the nine-block area of the city known as "the forest," meaning streets named after trees—Oak, Maple, Tulip, Elm, et cetera. Seven women, five men and six children—all unknown to one another—had been quite gruesomely dispatched in this area and all of the murders had taken place between 1:00 and 2:00 AM, the darkest hours of any day, and the hours when most people have fallen into a very deep sleep that's even deeper than REM sleep.

"You know what I think, Andrew?" he said: he had given up his 100mm cigarettes in favor of long, thin and not pleasingly aromatic cigars: he was punctuating his remarks by poking the air with one of these cigars and its acrid odor was making me feel nauseous.

"No," I said. "What do you think?"

"Well, I think these murders involve more than one person. That's what I think." He gave me a quizzical look. "Something wrong?"

I shook my head, put my hand to my mouth.

"Are you sick, Andrew?"

"Not really," I said and took my hand from my mouth.

He smiled. "You want to know why I think several people are involved in these murders?"

I nodded.

"Okay, I'll tell you." He leaned forward in his chair (we were seated at his comfy dining nook): he poked the disgusting cigar at me. "I think several people were involved because the victims themselves told me so." His smile became a shit-eating grin; he leaned back in his chair, nodded as if in agreement with himself, and added, "How do you like *them* apples, Andrew?"

I sighed.

He chuckled quickly. "Yeah, yeah, I know," he said. "The dead just *can't* speak to us. For Jesus Hopping Christ, if they *could* speak to us, they wouldn't be *the dead!*" He closed his eyes a moment, shook his head, and continued, "I've heard it all before. But they don't speak to *everyone*, Andrew. They speak only to those they feel they can trust."

"Like you?" I said.

He nodded earnestly. "Sure. Why not?"

"So I guess they don't trust *me*, and that's why they don't speak to me?" I said.

"Maybe they actually do trust you, Andrew. And maybe they actually *do* speak to you." He paused meaningfully. "Can you prove they don't?"

"Don't what?"

"Trust you." A pause. "*Speak* to you."

"Why would they?"

He shrugged. "Why indeed. Why does anyone, living or dead, or somewhere in between, trust and speak to anyone else?"

"I haven't the foggiest idea," I said. "Maybe you can enlighten me."

He gave me a flashy smile, inhaled deeply of his awful cigar, let the smoke amble from his mouth. "Well, I'll tell you why,

Andrew. Because they *have* to!" Brief pause. "They *have* to! Good Lord, they *have* to!"

If I were a real artist, I would have painted her again and again, in different poses and in different guises, in different places. I would have painted her naked in the woods and seated on a toilet and reading and dancing and knocking at my door.

I wasn't born in a 1967 Mercury Montclair. How would that have been possible, and how could you believe it? What's today's date, after all? Go and check. Have you returned? Good. Then you can see, shit, that not enough *time* (the great emancipator) has passed.

What are you, stupid?

Fred Spoon bleeped out of existence. Said again, "Good Lord, they *have* to!" and bleeped out of existence.

For now, within. My box of secrets.

ixiiiIXIiiiIXIS

leave the grieving
to the grievous

My father said this: "One does not sit on one's hands to grieve."
He was grieving my mother when he said it. So I said it, as well,
to a woman I didn't know, who was seated primly next to me at
the funeral home where Epistobel's consumable body had been
laid out, in violation of her privacy rights: I said, "One does
not sit on one's hands to grieve," and the woman seated next to
me—dark-haired, short, possessed of a championship nose and
dense eyelashes—said she'd like me to explain myself, so I said,
"It's something my father told me. I've repeated it to you verbatim.
I don't know what it means." The woman said her name was
Kathryn and that she was a friend of Epistobel's—though she
used Epistobel's actual name (which, even now, I don't remember), then added that she'd think about what I said, got up, paid
her final respects to Epistobel and, on the way out of the chapel,
touched my shoulder in a comforting way. I smiled up at her to
say thanks. She wasn't looking at me. I felt embarrassed.

⚿

Epistobel and I once had a late dinner at a fine Italian restaurant
called Mano del Giglio, just south of Corning, NY, where she

told me she knew, without a doubt, that she was going to lose me and that there was nothing she could do about it.

I told her, "That's a very odd thing to say, Epistobel."

She nodded, admitted that it was, indeed, a very odd thing to say, and that she had no choice but to say it, that it needed saying, that it was "in the cards," that it was something "fate has already worked out," and, at last, that it was best for both of us to go our separate ways after we had "enjoyed our dinner."

"Who can enjoy dinner, now?" I protested.

"Well, why can't we—in a place as fine as this," she said, and glanced about at the genuine Italian paintings and furnishings and wait people. "Look at it. So real."

"Of course it's real," I said.

"You're confused, I know," she said, and put her little hand on mine. "But, actually, you aren't. You must know that. And if you don't know it at this particular moment, you will know it before long and, because none of us has any choice but to cope with what is real, to live with it, and then, in time, to be done with it. You will, too, though you'll experience all there is of hell in the process."

What an awful way to spend our time together at such a fine restaurant, I thought.

She agreed.

"Yes, it is," she said. "But we have no choice."

As it turned out, she was right.

Hieronymus Bosch did some very nightmarish paintings, don't you think? He was a man caught up in endless turmoil, clearly he could eat his own soul, then vomit it up. I've done such things as that, though not at all with the same success, only to manipulate my manipulators, my benefactors, my detractors, those who are where I once was and who remain in places I cannot, anymore, even describe, let alone visit.

That, she says, *is the key to all happiness, now, Happy.*

across the lake in
the blue canoe and
then up the tall hill

And then, of course, to the little village or hamlet that exists there.

Which exists, I know, even at this moment, which is my endless moment.

Where I exist and speak of too many things, these things—the blue canoe, the tall hill, the little village or hamlet that exists there, the people who exist in it, who come and go like memories from building to building, through doors only they and I can use.

I have facts for you:

Pepsi's the real thing.

They also serve who only stand and wait.

If you have faith equal to a grain of mustard seed, you can move yourself off your dead ass and find happiness in more than just the mundane realm in which you took your first, desperate breath.

Love always waits.

You don't need to breathe to *be*.

It's cold everywhere in this universe.

A tiny investment in your future, now, will pay you back many fold. When the future arrives (which, I'm sorry, by definition, simply cannot happen), you'll be able to buy that vintage Chrysler you've always lusted after, or that fine pastel blue ranch house your parents lived and loved in.

Always make time to make time—you will be repaid by ten thousand or more orgasms in the span of a life.

Diamonds are a girl's best friend.

Always protect your orgasm.

Should you start to skid on an icy road, steer in the direction of the skid, unless your car has front-wheel drive, in which case you need to steer in the opposite direction of the skid.

It is always next to impossible, within a given desperate moment, to decide the direction of a skid.

Bodies deprived of breath decay at varying rates, depending on temperature, moisture, light, et cetera.

The dust in any occupied house is composed, primarily, of skin cells.

Contrary to popular literary usage, a few dead leaves still clinging to a tree in winter do not *shiver* in a cold wind; only mammals shiver.

Dead mammals do not shiver, however.

Bears are the only true hibernating mammals.

It is said, by some, perhaps by many, that when the dead on this planet outnumber the living then the dead (those who actually outnumber the living) will wander to and fro, from house to house, from village to restaurant, from shopping mall to drugstore to elementary schools and apartment buildings. And when they pass one another, the dead will nod and smile at each other and say, "I know you." They won't say this to the living because they simply will not know the living, and the living will not know them. How could they? Any of them.

⚷

Detective Fred Spoon came to me on a Wednesday morning that promised sleet and proclaimed in a loud and excited voice, "I've solved the tree-streets murders!"

"Have you?" I said.

"I have," he said.

"Tell me, then," I said.

"When I'm certain," he said, and loped back to his big Chrysler, got in, and roared off.

ixiiii

This is winter, and it seems the fox who lives above this oblong room was actually a vixen in estrous, for I have seen a number of fox cubs (also called "kits") trotting past my door in search of their mother and her bursting teats, or, perhaps, in search of other food, following the trail of odors nature has lain down for them.

Others have moved past my open door, as well. The bats, for instance—twice a day; at dusk and at dawn. And insects of various kinds. Deer, too. Such beautiful and graceful creatures. I've seen men, also. Dressed as if for the hunt. I've called to them, shouted curses at them, told them they're trespassing, that there is no hunting allowed here, but they've turned a deaf ear to me.

The clock chimes.

The clock chimes.

Here is a fact:

The chiming of a clock involves moments that cannot repeat, due to the constant and unceasing dissolution of subatomic particles.

Another fact:

The Big Dipper is the most recognizable of all constellations; the constellation Orion (in which the star Betelgeuse lies) is the second most recognizable. The Little Dipper is recognizable only to a few. Most people cannot name any other constellations, though there are hundreds. Over the span of many, many years, I have followed their movement across the heavens each night—weather allowing. I have found recently, however, that even on nights heavy with cloud, I can still see (albeit dimly) the constellations which bring me comfort, and also the moon in its various manifestations, and, if I look hard enough, the graceful spiral galaxy in the constellation of Andromeda, which is one million light years distant.

Here is a fact: one million light years equals approximately 6 and a half quadrillion miles. The world's fastest plane, traveling at, perhaps, 4000 miles per hour, would simply not be able to fly such a distance; its entire structure would disintegrate into molecules and atoms long before it even left the Milky Way.

This is a wondrous power I have—to see the great universe even through clouds—wouldn't you agree?

The clock chimes.

The comely young thing hasn't visited in many days and nights.

I hear people walking above me.

In this oblong room, my father hovers nearby like a huge dark bird with magnificent wings.

I can see my mother nowhere. It's possible, however, that, given enough time, I *will* see her. And perhaps, at last, I will know her as she wanted to be known.

Epistobel lies quiet and invisible beside me.

I hear her weeping often.

chapter one

If I hadn't been born, I would know it. How could I *not* know such a thing?

It is all that I do know, other than this: Eventually, I will find my way to the wondrous and graceful galaxy in Andromeda (then to the village or hamlet which exists there) in my blue canoe.

about the author

T.M. Wright—in his forty-eighth year as, in his words, "a writer in training"—has published 31 novels and novellas of, as he puts it, existential horror, numerous short stories and poems, and has created the cover art for several of his books, including this one. He's received lots of accolades from reviewers, readers, and other writers who shall here remain nameless because the book you hold in your hands must, like anything a writer writes, speak for itself. His best books are his latest, he says—*The Eyes of the Carp* (Cemetery Dance, 2005), *A Spider On My Tongue* (Nyx Books, 2006), and the widely acclaimed *I Am the Bird* (PS Publishing, 2006).

Look for his first collection of short stories, a novel, poetry and art, *Bone Soup*, from Cemetery Dance late in 2009.